Prologue

~1975 Detroit Michigan~

(Yelling from outside Brothel)

As the man pushed the woman on to the ground and got on top of her smushing his hands into her face. The woman was able to take his two fingers and bite down as hard as she could and kneed him in his balls to defend herself. As he fell to the ground, she then climbed on top of him and begun to fight back. While delivering punches to his face while tears rolled from eyes enjoying the satisfaction of pain conflicted back on to him. As she continued to punch, kick and even spit on him, she came to a clear decision that she was tired of him. That she was every woman that a man could ever want and love and would like to be free. While the woman's husband laid on the sidewalk holding his chest and wiping the blood from his lip with the collar of his T-shirt. She then stood over him while pulling out a divorce settlement for him to sign, while shouting from the top her lungs "sign me my fucking rights."

As the woman slapped the papers in his face and walked away, the woman's husband continued to lay back on to the concrete and cry while holding on to the signed document. Once the man has received help getting up from off the ground by someone walking by, he then stumbles and limps his way back up the steps of the Brothel home. As he was about to reach the top of the staircase Juanita closes the curtains to the windows and replied "ok we have seen enough, someone please stop that negro from coming back in here. As two women ran towards the door, they placed their foot in the doorway blocking his entrance into the home. When he seen that they blocked him from gaining any entrance back into the home, he started to become loud and obnoxious with the women and started to call them out of their names. As the women called security to come back up to the front of the home to deescalate the problem, Juanita decided to call off security and take matters into her own hands.

Overhearing the commotion that he has started with the other women, Juanita made her way to the front door and said "negro I'm just trying to figure out what part of no you can't enter that you don't get!" As she told her girls to step to aside and have stepped to him face to face, he remained quiet. Juanita laughs and replies "cat must got your tongue, "what happened to all that shit you was talking sucker?" Roy tries to explain himself "Juanita baby look I got money to pay for a few more services; a few more rounds with the girls won't hurt." As he tried to push her out the way to get back inside, she then shoved him back on to the porch and delivered a slap to his face. While shouting what a disgrace he was "Maybe you should take your ass home, your bruised up you look a mess, and my girls are already satisfied with the amount of money you offered them." Roy touches the left side of his face "so it's like that huh", Juanita stands with her hands on her hips "and what else it's supposed to be like?" As Roy stared down Juanita, he then sucked his teeth and backed away slowly holding on to his breeches. As he walked down the steps with his backed turned towards the road Juanita replied "sorry Roy we just don't need any trouble around these parts. As he found her words hard to receive, he then sucked his teeth once some more and called her bitch while walking off.

While Juanita made her way back into the home and shook her head while taking a deep breathe. She then headed down to her quarters to count up the money that the women have brought in for the night. As she counted the stacks suddenly there were knocks at the front door and excessive amounts of mashing of the doorbell. As the other women of the home were busy entertaining their fellas for the rest of the night. Juanita have gotten up from her chair and went to answer the door "I'm coming damn how many times you going to make all of that ruckus." As Juanita made it to the door and opened it, she quickly tried to shut the door as she seen who were there to visit her. As she pushed the door and begun to scream out for help out came the others from servicing their clients, wondering what could have been going on. As Juanita struggled with pinning her back up against the door she shouted "five 0, five 0 come get ahold of this door with me." While the girls stood in confusion and fear for their life, they quickly ran over to the door and pinned their backs up against it. While the others went to check to see if all the windows and back doors were locked.

Once the other women went to check the windows in came a can of tear gas that was tossed in from the window and landed on the floor of the waiting area. As the gas was released into the air and the girls begun to scream and fall into walls screaming about their eyes. Juanita have quickly let go of the door and rushed to see what was happening with them. As she turned the corner to the waiting area and seen them kicking and screaming, she whispered silently under her voice "no not my girls what the fuck." While she stood in complete shock in came the police barging through the home knocking down the other females and cuffing them into handcuffs. As the police tried their best to cuff some of them, some of the women have fought back and have ran out of the back door.

While the authorities have shouted for everyone to place their hands behind their backs and to remain silent. The women of the Brothel have refused to listen and placed hand's on every police officer that tried to use excessive force with them. When Juanita seen how dangerous it was becoming and saw one of her girls getting punched in the face by one of the officers. She quickly rushed over to him and begun to grab his face from behind and scratched him. As she held tightly to his eyelids an officer quickly snuck up behind her and hit her in the back with a nightstick. Once the nightstick connected with her back, she screamed, while the officer snatched her by her hair and grabbed a hold of both of her arms to cuff her. Once she was placed in handcuffs, she was dragged out of the home backwards and told that she was being arrested for running an illegal Brothel and that the community has voted to shut it down.

Chapter 1. Idea's

~March 2022~Porters' coffee shop- Friday 12pm

Pressing her lips against the coffee cup and smelling the sweet smell of hazelnut brewed into several cups. Sipped Fallon as she sat with her legs crossed in a black leather bikers' jacket. "Girl, you know I am about sick of you" said Dominique, Fallon laughs "what, what did I do now?" said Fallon. Dominique bats her eyes and twists her face towards her jacket. "Honey it's the jacket for me it's given' I miss Johnathan" said Dominique, Lori chuckles as she takes a quick sip of her margarita. Fallon takes a sip of her coffee then places the cup down on to the table as she reacts "really Dom really?", Dominique reacts back "hey I'm just saying." Lori continues to chuckle at both going back in forth "so are you insinuating that she misses her ex", Dominique responds in laughter "clearly this girl never goes anywhere without his jacket." As Fallon bit into her scone and rolled her eyes at her, she then told Lori that she may need a sip of her margarita to gather her quickly. Lori and Dominique both laughed at Fallon as she jokingly said, "girl mind your business that's all you need to do is just mind your business."

As Dominique sat back and waited for an answer Fallon then placed a smirk on her face and said, "ok guys I'm going to be real as possible, no I don't miss Johnathan so that question is out the window, but me and Johnathan have been." Dominique reacts in shock "nooo, are you and Johnathan still fucking!" Lori taps Dominique on the arm "girl let her finish, go ahead girl because I got to hear this." As Fallon finished off her coffee, she then winked at both while popping the collar of her jacket and replied, "we are fucking hard." Dominique and Lori bursts into a big scream while laughing "bitch wait, so Johnathan is still laying that pipe?" said Lori. Fallon responds, "more like I'm laying the Coochie; although we are not together, I still get him to jump and do for me when it's necessary." Dominique laughs and daps her up "okay boss bitch, put that nigga to work", "look at you, wearing the brothers' jacket and giving him some pussy keep it up that ass going to be pregnant," said Lori. While Lori and Dominique joked around with her and continued to laugh, Fallon then laughed with them and replied "never, that nigga wouldn't stand a chance."

As Fallon signaled for the waiter to bring over the checkbook, she then took one more bite out of her steak omelet. "Wait a minute you're not leaving already, are you?" said Dominique. Fallon puts down her fork and opens the checkbook to find her total and replied, "that I am babes a girl has some business to take care of." Lori places her elbows upon the table with her fist placed under her chin "ooow, please do tell me more", Fallon looks over at Lori and responded, "girl you are so nosey, all I am doing is heading over to my mommas house to give her a hand with cleaning." Dominique throws up her hands "oh my gosh please don't tell me momma Joyce is still paranoid about covid", "girl have you told her that the numbers of active cases have went down," said Lori. Fallon signs off on her receipt while shrugging her shoulders "I tried but you both know that my momma is set in her ways; it's hard getting through that woman and plus she's a daily watcher she possibly knows more than me." Dominique and Lori both shook their heads as they laughed about momma Joyce, "well next time when we get up for friend and teatime you will order a margarita instead of a cup of coffee" Dominique Insisted. Fallon reaches in for a hug "okay ok next time I'll have a margarita for lunch" said Fallon, "you sure will, make that two," said Lori. Fallon chuckles as she replied, "ok you drunks", as Fallon hugged both girls and said her goodbyes, she then headed down to the nearest corner market to pick up some supplies.

As she entered the market she then walked over to the back shelf and placed a pack of sponges, bleach and some dish soap into her basket. While she headed up to the counter to make her purchase, she then notices a book that listed real estate properties for sale. As she picked up the book and begun to flip through the pages, she then came to a page with a property that stood out to her. While the clerk started to become impatient with her by shouting "any day now" Fallon quickly dropped the book into the basket and made sure that the clerk rung it up with the rest of her items. While Fallon grabbed a hold of her bags and stepped outside of the market, she then reached down into one of the sacks and pulled out the book of listings. As she skimmed through the book to search for the property that she was looking for. She then came to the page of the property and typed the location into her phone to start her search. As she ridden the bus over to the area of the home, she then walked a couple of blocks over from where the bus has dropped her off up to the house.

Once Fallon spotted out the house she then walked across the road and stood in front of the home. As she stood viewing the home, she then took another look into her book of listings and said to herself in a cheerful voice "this is it." As she became excited about the home, she quickly made her way up the steps and peeped in between all the windows that were visible to the inside of the home. As she peeped into the home, she seen that the home was in poor condition and that renovations have not been taking place. That the home was in complete distress and gave off a shabby appearance that would turn away any buyer that are interested. As Fallon viewed all that she could have viewed of the home, she then headed back down the staircase and turned towards the home to take one more look. While she stood gazing at the home, coming up the opposite side of the road was a woman by the name Susan McCain. As Susan seen her staring at the home, she became uneased and decided to let her presence be known.

Standing across the way Susan have caught Fallon's attention "some home huh?", Fallon turns and looks at her "yes big if you ask me." As Susan stood holding her purse in close to her, she then replied, "now what would you do with a home that size." Fallon smiled at the woman and responded, "well I guess I would purchase it for me, but by the listing price set at $500,000 that's a little steep." As Susan smirked back at Fallon she then replied, "well to help you out just a little, there's always a home for rent down in the lower areas of the city where it's more suitable for folks like yourself if the price is an issue." As Fallon turned and looked back at Ms. McCain she then quickly responded with disappointment and confusion "wait what you say?" As Susan placed her hand out in front of her, she then said, "pardon me but I hope you don't plan on having any outrages idea's when you settle for this home; like running a whore house like the last owner." As Fallon stood quietly in shock Susan then said, "us conservative women of our community will not stand for it and what happened to the sexualized women in 1975 was bad, but we stand for our rights." As Fallon sucked her teeth and rolled her eyes at Susan McCain she then said, "you know what you white motherfuckers always walk around here with your heads-up high thinking that you run shit; when all you do is steal keep the poor in poverty and continue to make the rich wealthier." As Susan tried to speak, Fallon then dismissed her by saying "Susan thank you for your uninvited time and remember that my money can stretch as far as yours and buy up as many properties as it wants." As Susan stood holding her purse tightly against her waist, she then became upset and walked off once she seen two Black males heading down the same sidewalk as her. While Fallon stood watching her walk away, she then turned back to the house and smiled saying to herself "damn what type of history you hold."

    As Fallon finished up viewing the home, she then headed to her mother's house to help her with her deep cleaning. As Fallon walked through the front door of the home there was Joyce sitting on the sofa waiting for her patiently. Momma Joyce replied, "it's about time you showed up!", as Fallon stood holding the bag of supplies up against her chest. She then looked at her and said, "well dang momma hi to you to", as Fallon walked down the hall into the kitchen. Joyce then risen from the sofa and made her way in behind her saying "I thought you wasn't coming you know an elderly lady like myself tends to get inpatient waiting long periods of time." Fallon turns to her and rolls her eyes while laughing "well I'm here now momma I just had some places to be before I made my way over here; don't worry yourself so much." While Fallon was pulling out the supplies Joyce then sat down at the kitchen table and said, "I sure do miss your father sometimes it can get lonely at times; I know that if he was here, we would be off somewhere in the islands." Fallon laughs "isn't that the truth he definitely made sure that you guys got to experience something different; blessed you both with amazing trips." As Joyce sat reminiscing the good times her and her husband shared, Fallon then comforts her while saying "momma you have nothing to worry about although daddy is gone, he left a soldier behind, I'll take care of you."

While Fallon delivered a hug and a kiss on the forehead of her mother, she then insisted that she must get cleaning. As Fallon begun to do the dishes and started to toss away any food from the fridge and cabinet that were outdated. Her mother then asked about her wellbeing "so if you don't mind me asking how's everything going with you?" Fallon responds, "well so far so good I really can't complain, just living life day by day", as Momma Joyce side eyed her. She then happened to walk over to a black box that sat high upon a spice rack in the corner of the kitchen and pulled out some cash. As she pulled out the cash she then walked up behind Fallon and offered her to take the money. As Fallon stopped washing the dishes and turned towards her, she then looks down at her mother's hand and refused "I'm sorry momma but I can't take that." Momma Joyce stood in wonder "and why not don't you see I'm trying to bless you", Fallon sighs "that's perfectly fine momma but you need it more than I do please hold on to your money." As momma Joyce continued to beg her to take the money, Fallon then politely said "momma I love you, but you have done enough already." While Fallon turned back around and went back to cleaning the dishes momma Joyce then stood still behind her and said, "I can tell when something is bothering you or when something isn't right." When Fallon finished drying the last dish and placed it into the cabinet, she then turned to Joyce and held on to her shoulders "momma I'm fine the least thing I need you to do is to stress over me."

While Joyce stood still looking into Fallon's eyes, she then looked at the money in her hands and placed it back into the jar above the spice rack. When she placed the money into the jar, she then took a moment to gather her thoughts and have let out a big sigh. As Fallon moved on to the next cleaning task, Joyce then turned to her and said, "I know that you're not working." As Fallon came to a pause and dipped the mop back into the bucket she then replied "momma, how do you know that?" Joyce shakes her head and shouts "your sister told me, she also told me you needed to borrow $200.00 as well." Fallon stands in disbelief while mumbling under her breath "I swear that girl has never been able to hold water," said Fallon. As Fallon stood with her arms folded momma Joyce then replied, "I know that times are rough right now, but you need to be working or doing something with your life; how about going back to school and getting a master's degree like your sister." Fallon frowns up her face towards her comment "I don't need no degree to determine how great I am and what works for Ray doesn't work for everyone else." Momma Joyce replies, "I'm just saying?", "and I'm just saying too, I'm not Ray" shouted Fallon, "I'm my own person what happened to us being able to embrace our talents and our ability to strive individually, isn't that what you preached? All I am saying is that I couldn't help that I got laid off because of covid."

As Joyce stood quietly listening to her, she then took a seat at the kitchen table and replied, "so what's next for you?" Fallon sighed and said, "I really don't know but whatever it is, I know that I'm going to be great at it." As Joyce have taken Fallon by the hand, she begun to spread positivity into the atmosphere and asked God to cover her and to bless her abundantly. "You're going to be fantastic my daughter" said Joyce, as Fallon let go of her hand, she then looked up at the spice jar and said, "momma I'm about to head out before it gets too late; but before I do, I was wondering?" Before Fallon was able to finish her sentence momma

Joyce put up her hand and begun to crack a smile at her, while given her the permission to do so "go right ahead it's all yours." As Fallon grabbed a hold of the money, she then thanked her mother with a kiss on the forehead and left her with a cryptic message before heading out of the home "you know you are a strong woman but even sometimes a strong woman tends to fall weak, know that all trophies don't come neatly polished, sometimes they carry stains.

While Fallon walked away from her mother leaving her speechless, off she went heading home to be in her own space. As she arrived back home and took one step inside, she then placed her purse down on to the nearest sofa and reached for the light switch. As she found the switch and flicked the switch upwards, she then shouted "what the fuck" as she noticed that the lights have been shut off. As Fallon continued to flick the switch and test out the other switches in the home, she then placed her hands upon her head and said to herself "this can't be happening right now." While Fallon stood with her hands upon her head she then thought about where she kept all her bills and went on a search to find them. As Fallon searched the back of the home first and then made her way towards the front, she then thought to check the mail that she tossed on the kitchen counter, the day that she was in a rush for a job interview. As Fallon entered the kitchen and scrambled through the mail, she then found an envelope that was mailed from the electric company. Warning her that she has ten days to make a payment, or they will be forced to stop service. As Fallon glued her eyes to the bill she then mumbled under her breath "shit what am I going to do now."

As Fallon placed the bill to the side of her and looked at her phone, she then begun to sigh while taking a deep breath to ease her frustrations. As she picked up her phone and viewed her contact list, she then said to herself "what use is he to have around if I'm not going to use him." As Fallon took another deep breath in, she then dialed the number and waited patiently for an answer. While the other line picked up, Fallon quickly responded in a sexy tone "Hey Johnathan, baby I was wondering if you could give me a hand tonight; somethings came up and I really can use your help, so are you free?" As Fallon waited for his response she then paused and looked at the phone and said "hello." While Fallon sat listening to the background of the call, a woman then replied, "who is this and what do you want with Johnathan." As Fallon stood in shock and remained speechless looking down at the phone, the woman then said, "there's no need to be silent." As Fallon asked to speak to Johnathan the woman behind the other line handed over the phone and went back to lying in bed.

As Johnathan took over the call Fallon then replied, "I guess this happens to be wrong timing?" Johnathan sucks his teeth "yea, you right but what's up." Fallon takes one more glance at the outstanding balance and replied, "it's my lights they shut me off, apparently they have sent out a notice, but I guess somehow I overlooked the bill; so, I missed the deadline." As Fallon stood with her hands in her pockets waiting for a response from Johnathan she then replied, "no answer nor offer." Johnathan then looked back at the woman lying in bed and said in a low tone "I guess you got to figure it out", Fallon begins to raise her voice "what do you mean!? You always come through for me what's so different about now," said Fallon. Johnathan quickly replies, "I don't have to explain the difference, you already know what it is." Fallon rolls her eyes and leans over the counter while holding the phone up closely to her ear in a sexy voice "you know I'm the only one that can stroke them balls and give it to you the way you truly want it; you know our love for each other still runs deep." As Johnathan listened to every word, she was saying he then told her to stop "I think you're missing the big picture." In curiosity Fallon wonders what he was referring to "what picture could I be missing when I only see one", Johnathan sighs then responds, "Fallon give it up, I already know why you like having me around."

Fallon leans up from against the counter and laughs as she responds, "boy what are you talking about?" As Johnathan have jumped up from the side of the bed and walked out of the bedroom. He then held the phone up closely to his ear and replied in a low tone, "Fallon I'm going to ask you to move on with your life; I'm done, we been broken up for three months now and all I see is that you think that I'm your personal A.T.M." As Fallon holds on to the chain around her neck and takes a hard swallow. She then became upset with him rolled her eyes and replied, "so that trick over there must really be blowing you good huh?" as Johnathan was about to respond back to Fallon. In came the other woman standing behind him dressed in a mesh robe clearing her throat, as Johnathan realized that she wasn't too happy about him being on the phone with Fallon. He then hung up the phone and headed over to her wrapping his arms around her waist as she delivered a kiss to his lips. As Fallon heard the call drop, she then stood shouting to herself "oh no he didn't, I know this bitch don't have all his attention" as Fallon decided to place another call out to Johnathan, she received no answer. While she stood not knowing what her next move was, she became frustrated and slammed the phone on to the kitchen counter and walked off. As Fallon walked off from the kitchen in anger and disappointment, she then stopped herself in the middle of the hall and looked at her purse. As she stood staring at the purse on top of the counter, she then walked over and begun to search through it. While Fallon went through the purse and pulled out the $200.00 that was giving to her. She then looked over at the notice and back at the money and snatched both from off the counter while walking back to the bedroom slamming the door shut behind her.

Chapter 2. You want it you got it

~Conservative leadership committee~

(Phone rings) "Hey are you going to get that?" as Grace looked over at her coworker she then replied, "I wish sometimes you will just mind your business." As Grace picked up the phone to answer the call she then replied "good day at C.L.C how may I take your call, hello, hello, thank you for calling C.L.C." As Grace noticed that nobody was answering on the opposite end of the line, she then placed the phone back on the hook. While Grace went back to filing her nails and chewing her gum with her feet propped up on the desk. In came Katherine Watson knocking her two feet down from off the desk saying in a sharp tone "little lady I don't know what you are doing or where you believe you are at; this is not a resort this is work and I expect you to act like it." As Grace looked up at Katherine in disgrace she then mumbled underneath her breath "a resort would be lovely then being trapped in an office filled with uptight folks." As Katherine overheard her mumbling underneath her breath she then replied, "well if you feel that way there's the door make sure it doesn't t hit you on your way out; but as of now I have a job for you to fulfill." As Mrs. Watson grabbed a hold of a box that she sat beside her on the floor, she then picked back up the box and dropped it into Graces lap and told her to "get shredding."

As Grace looked down at the box and viewed the papers that needed shredded, she then said, "Mrs. Watson but this can take all day." Mrs. Watson begins to laugh "all day you say! Well looks like you have your work cut out for today." As Grace took one more look into the box at the massive paper load, she then sat back in her seat to take a few breaths. As Mrs. Watson stood at the counter snapping her fingers to get her attention she then replied, "today I need you to be sure to forward every message to my office; I'll be conducting a meeting with my fellow colleagues, so please do not disturb if you do, you'll be fired." As Mrs. Watson turned her back towards Grace, she then walked down the hall into a conference room. Once she entered the room there was half of the staff sitting around a wooded oval shaped table waiting for her appearance. As she made her way over to her seat, she then let her colleagues know that they have lots' to cover for the day. As she took her seat at the head of the table, she then opened a red folder and told everyone to look at page five.

While everyone sat reading to themselves, she then begun to see the disgusting looks upon their faces and said out loud "shameful article isn't it." As all the colleagues sat in disappointment and agreed with her, they all begun to voice their opinions all at once. As one woman stood from her seat in such rage, she then shouted out how unfair the other party was and how they are the cause for democracy in America. While Mrs. Watson amongst the other colleagues listened to the woman voice her opinion. Katherine then told the woman that she may be seated and went on to say that America was being corrupted and oversaturated with citizens that admires the views of a democrat. As everyone that sat around the table shaken their heads and frowned up their faces towards the conversation. Mrs. Watson then replied, "them donkeys wouldn't dare to stand a chance to go up against us republicans, us conservative women we got what it takes, we have guts, and we will get the votes of the people when the time is right."

As Katherine Watson stood up from her seat before the people, she then raised up her right hand and swore to the committee that she will help spread the awareness amongst abortions in their community. As Mrs. Watson took her seat, the committee then came up with a clever idea to start spreading the word by holding a rally at a local community center in the heights of the city. When she sat and listened to every idea that came to her colleague's mind, she then told them to write it down until that day comes. As Mrs. Watson sat back in her seat with a smirk upon her face she then said, "you know what be sure to write down that the rally would also feature a picnic style lunch, you never could go wrong with food." As the fingers of her colleagues begun to write down everything that she expects for the rally to be. She then sat up straight in her seat and intended to move on to their next topic of the day. Until Susan grabbed her attention by clearing her throat and whispering in closely that she needed to speak with her. As Katherine turned and looked at Susan she then whispered, "would it be possible that it could wait until after the meeting?" Susan refuses as she shakes her head no and responded "this, you may want to add to the meeting." As Susan sat up straight in her chair and shook her head in disgrace. Katherine then replied, "Susan could you please inform us on what you would like for me to add into our meeting on today," as Susan taking a hard swallow.

She then looked around the table at every individual and back at Katherine and said in disappointment "The Berkley house is back on the market." As Mrs. Watson spat up her coffee on to a napkin that sat beside her. She insisted that everyone should take a fifteen minute break by ushering them outside of the room with her hands while she shuts and locks the door behind her. As she locked her and Susan in the conference room together, she then asked for Susan to repeat herself, once Susan repeated with what was going on with the Berkley house. Katherine then wanted to know where she has received her information from and wondered how long the property has been listed. "That house has been foreclosed on ever since 1975 there's no way that the home would be able to be listed without the committees votes nor my stamp of approval," said Mrs. Watson. As Mrs. Watson placed her coffee cup back to the base of her lips to take another sip, Susan then told her about the for sale sign that stood in front of the home and about the young woman that was wandering on the front porch. "There was a for sale sign and also a woman, a Black woman at that; she seemed highly interested in the property when I spoking to her, I tried to scare her off, but she wouldn't back down," said Susan McCain.

While Watson put down her coffee cup and walked over to the brochure table to check the paper to see which homes were for sale in the area. She then asked if she knew who was responsible, for placing the home back on the market "Any idea on who is deciding to sale this property?" Susan quietly stood in the back of her while taking a deep breath saying "yes, but I don't think you are going to be too thrilled about who is over the property." Katherine turns and responds to Susan "I suppose, but why would I ?! that property holds so much tarnishing memories of women that sold their bodies just for a hot meal and a place to stay." Susan replies, "which happens to be a disgrace to humanity" "right, now who is it?" asked Mrs. Watson. As Mrs. Watson placed down the newspaper back on to the brochure table, demanding Susan to tell her who was the agent over the Berkley Estates. Susan then cracked under pressure and revealed the mystery person "it's Brad, Brad Watson." As Susan revealed the agent over the Berkley Estates, Mrs. Watson then stood with an unpleasant look on her face saying "well it seems as Mr. Brad Watson would have a lot of explaining to do."

Once Mrs. Watson thanked Susan McCain for sharing the news that she gathered from her walk to work. She then grabbed ahold of her binder and her coffee cup, while she ranted to Susan about how he has messed up big time. As Mrs. Watson passed by Susan on her way out of the conference room, Susan then stops her while saying "I know that you may be upset but trust me I'm sure you don't have anything to worry about; Brad is for sure not going to sale to no nigger." As Mrs. Watson came to a pause at the door to exit the conference room. She then turns around and walks up to Susan and delivers a hard smack across her face that all Susan McCain could do is look up at her in shock. While Susan stood holding the left side of her face Mrs. Watson then replied, "how dare you fix your mouth to call another race such a trash word." As Susan took the tips of her fingers and ran it across her face over the redness of the cheek. Mrs. Watson then told her that she was fired and to leave the premises immediately and to never step foot back into the office. As Susan took off in a hurry out of the conference room Mrs. Watson then followed behind making her way down the hall to confront Mr. Brad Watson.

~Brad Watson's office suite 4c~

Barging through the doorway into republic reality and into Mr. Watson office, Katherine stood boldly in front of his desk waiting for him to finish his phone call to address him about the Berkley Estates. As Mr. Watson conversation between him and his client have seemed to not come to an end anytime soon. Katherine wasted no time unplugging the phone line from the phone jack to grab his attention. As Katherine tossed the cord on to the floor and stomped her right foot over it Mr. Watson then dropped the phone and stood up shouting "honey what the hell was that about, that was an important call." As Katherine walks from around the desk and stands face to face with Mr. Watson. She then delivers a hard smack across his face while yelling "you asshole how could you, how could you do this to me." As Katherine goes in for another slap, Brad then catches her arm and tells her to not swing again. Once Katherine pulled her arm back from Brad she then shouts "you sure been having a lot of tricks up your sleeves; did you think that I wasn't going to find out." Brad sighs while responding "this must be about the Berkely Estates", "your damn sure right it is, The Berkley Estates that my mother fought hard to shut down and to never be placed on the market again," said Katherine.

As Brad turns his back towards Katherine and heads over to his desk to take a seat Katherine then shouted "I will not allow you to sale what use to be a whore house to any god forsaken body; that home has been ruled out and can only surpass by votes by our approval." As Brad listened to Katherine ramble on about her mother's wishes and the conservative committee rules, he then stopped her by saying "a half of a million is what we are settling for; don't tell me you want me to turn down this deal." As Katherine stood silently thinking about the money that is being offered for the home, she then shook her head and replied "as much that I want to support your decision, I'm sorry but I will not acknowledge." As Brad sat back in his chair while lighting a cigarette, he then cut his eye at her and laughed underneath his breath. As she watched him take a few puffs she then replied "I guess I'm not the only one that's stressed" Brad chuckles "stress! what could you be stressed about?"

While Katherine placed her left hand upon her head and sighed deeply, she then told him about the termination of Susan. Saying "it was meant to happen", as Brad rose from his seat and walked over to her holding her by her waist. She then replied "I learned a lot being married to you, I would have never thought that I would have to get rid of someone because of the words they choose to describe somebody." As Brad held her by her waist tight and delivered a kiss to her forehead he then replied "you didn't do it for you; you did it for him." Once Brad let go of Katherine and headed out of the office to grab lunch, Katherine then stood to herself holding back tears as it was hard for her to accept his words leaving her speechless.

~Fallon's Apartment~

As the morning done set in there was Fallon rumbling through a dresser draw for her last pack of blunt wrappers. When she found them, she grabbed ahold of two and begun to grind up some weed so she can wake in bake. Fallon was a firm believer in wake and bake culture she felt that every roll was necessary in order to get through her day. As she placed the blunt to her lips and laid back on to the bed to relax in came a call from her good friend Dominique. As she answered the phone she laughed and responded with "now bitch what level of high you on because I'm just now getting started." Dominique chuckles and replies, "Gurl I'm on that second wave and loving it hunty." As Dominique fell back on to her bed and kicked her two feet in excitement, she then told Fallon to hold as she was about to add Lori to the line. Once Lori was added to the line Fallon then asked "so Lori my gurl now what type of high is your ass on because I know you be having that good shit." As Lori begun laughing while inhaling the marijuana smoke, she then replied with "I guess you can already tell by the way I almost choked on that motherfucker, my ass is on that third wave of that good o sour."

As Dominique and Fallon busted out into laugher, Lori then became curious of what they were smoking on "so what yall niggas smoking on." Fallon replies, "man this them Skittles, and we definitely not tasting no rainbow but we sure is going to touch it", "that's right," shouted Dominique. "So, what you hoe's have plan for today?" asked Lori, Dominique replies "nothing except for this job; that I can't stand", "what about you Fallon" asked Lori. As Fallon sat up and placed her back against the headboard taking two puffs of her blunt, she then replied in excitement "well let's just say your girl isn't clocking into anyone's time clock today." "OH, is that so; but you are off to somewhere today though?" asked Lori. As Fallon chuckled underneath her breath she then gave in and told them about her new adventure "so guys I been doing my research and I have come to a decision on what I'm going to do with these stacks." As Lori and Dominique jumped in excitement ready to hear Fallon's next move. Fallon then replied "this bitch here is about to be her own boss; because I'm about to make these dollar bills rain down on the Berkley Estates."

Lori laughs "Ha, ha, ha wait sis wait I'm sorry for laughing but are you talking about the Berkley Estates the historic legendary whore house; the Ms. Fabulous Juanita." Fallon cracks a smile and begins to chuckle while saying "damn girl you are on it; yes, I read the back history on it and all I can think about is how messed up them crooked ass cops and they washed up nosey ass cracker bitches were." "If she was still up and running, I bet you that her name would run heavy in these streets," said Lori. As Fallon sat quietly and took another hit of her joint with a smirk on her face she then replied back to Lori "oh it will, but the only difference is that there's a new sheriff in town and this one isn't to be fucked with." "Are you serious, is this what you really been saving up for to start an escorting business; I was really convinced that you left that shit alone," shouted Dominique. As Fallon frowned up her face at the phone, she then replied back to Dominque saying "and I thought you have left a lot of shit alone as well to; but I see you still getting your money from elsewhere because we all know that Terrence sure can't afford it."

As Lori continued to smoke her blunt and defuse the tension between Fallon and Dominique over the phone. Dominique then replied "well at lease my utilities are paid, and my hair stay laid. "Ugh, bitch you make me sick" shouted Fallon, "look guys we all been there before we all escorted who gives a fuck if one of us wants to go back to being that; Dominique chill dude like you doing too much," said Lori. Fallon then weighs in "yeah seems like ever since you moved uptown you forgot where the fuck you came from, them unlock doors and cold floors let's not forget about them times." As Dominique sat quietly in her feelings, she then hung up the phone on both Lori and Fallon. While they both have remained on the line Lori then asked Fallon when she was going to make an offer, as Fallon thought about a perfect time she then replied "today at the showing" with a smile upon her face.

~The Berkley Estates~

Once Fallon set in her mind that she was going to view the property and make an offer she wasted no time on doing just that. As she dressed from head to toe in a white blouse, casual blue denim jeans with a cream heel. While she strutted her way up to the home, she paused for a second and taking a look at the realtor sign and crossed her fingers for good luck. As she entered the home there was a man by the name David Cohan, David was one of Brad Watson's right hand guys to get the job done. While she stood looking around at all the damage that was done to the place, she then happens to clear her throat to let him know that she was there. As David greeted her with a handshake and a warming smile he then replied "welcome, welcome you must be here to view the home I hope you are excited because this is one that features everything that you could want."

As she gazed her eyes around the home she then replied "I thought there would be other people lined up to see this property since it suppose to be so special." David places his two hands into his pockets and cracks a smirk "yea we were pushing for a bigger crowd to fill in one of these time slots but apparently due to the poor condition it's in and the crazy stigma around it I'm sure nobody is really interested; but hey we have you right?" As Fallon gives David a funny look then cuts her eyes over at a vanity that sat in the corner of the great room. She then cut her eye back at him and replied "sure, I think I can consider that", as David was happy to hear that she was interested in viewing the home. He then showed her around first starting off with what use to be a dining hall then further down the hall to view the kitchen and 7 bedrooms. As they came to a stop in what was known as the master suite, he then wanted to know her opinion on the home "so what do you think?"

    While Fallon stood wondering why would he even ask her a question like that she then replied "you can't be serious in all honesty sir this place looks like a piece of shit." David becomes nervous and starts to feel upset "I knew you was going to say that; I wish Brad would have listened to me when I said that nobody is going to want to buy this property. As Fallon stuck out her hand in front of him to stop him from speaking, she then said to him "whoever said I was not interested I just said that it was a piece of shit." David begins to become excited "wait so are you telling me your settling" Fallon smirks at David "it's a fixer upper but who said that the girl is not built for the challenge, so yes I consider the offer." As David became ecstatic about her agreeing to owning the home, he then told her that he would love for her to meet with Brad to discuss furthermore information about the home and to sign off for ownership. As he told her to give him a minute while he makes the call out to Brad. She then steps foot out on to the porch of the home and waits patiently, once he was done with the call, he then handed her the address to Mr. Watsons office and wished her the best of luck.

    As Fallon took the information that David gave to her to meet with Brad Watson, she wasted no time heading over to his office to claim her new home. As she made it to the office she then casually walked over to the receptionist and told her to let him know that his 10:00 appointment with Fallon Harris has arrived. Once the receptionist has buzzed Mr. Watson, he then gave the ok for her to allow Ms. Harris to continue walking down to his office. While Fallon did just that eyes from the cubicles and other rooms that were passed appeared to be glued to her. As they watched her as she walked down to the big man's office, as she made it to his office. There he was dressed to impress in the best tailored made business suit you can ever find in the city of Detroit. As he sat behind his desk writing in his notepad he happened to look up and notice Fallon standing at the door.

In shock Brad welcomes her in with a warm smile and a handshake "nice to meet you I'm Brad Watson you must be Fallon Harris." As Fallon shook his hand and sat down across from him at his desk. He wasted no time jumping into why she was there, "so you are interested in the Berkley Estates property I heard," said Brad. As Fallon sat with her back straight up in the chair she then replied "yes that is why I am here." As Brad smiled at Fallon, he then said to her "smart move I been looking forward to someone settling on this home for a few weeks now, and I have to say you're going to love it." "Even with the run down walls, the broken windows and the scraped up floors?" asked Fallon. Brad chuckles "well see all of that is repairable and I'm sure it could be handled by a girl that's up for the challenge." As Brad printed out the form for her to fill out for the home with the cash balance of how the home would be paid in full. She then happened to sign her name at the bottom of the form and slid it back to him. As Brad taking a look at the form he then replied "wait what's up with these numbers this home is being sold off for a half a million."

As Fallon looked over at him and chuckled underneath her breath she then replied "and that I'm aware of, but how can you make something profitable when it's looks doesn't appeal to its value so I say $290,000 or no deal." While Brad looked down at the paper and back up at her he then placed a smile upon his face and replied "I really like you Ms. Harris and I think that you are a smart lady but that offer is just not an offer that I can come to an agreement on I apologize." As Fallon rose from her seat, she thanked Mr. Watson for his time and headed for the door. As Mr. Watson stops her, he then asked her what was it that he can do to make her consider his offer. As Fallon stood at the doorway and thought about it, she then told him that he would need to agree to himself and the company providing the renovations and that he, sales the home as a commercial site instead of a home. As Brad was about to respond back to

Fallon in came Katherine Watson barging in and giving both the side eye. As Fallon headed out of his office, Katherine then turns to him and asked "so what was you guys discussing?", Brad responds "well if you would like to know, she was actually here to purchase one of our newest homes down in the renaissance district; but we ran into a credit issue so she is off to try someone else." As Katherine smiled at Brad she then replied "ok well I guess I'll go back to minding my business but before I do; I wanted to let you know that we have been invited to dinner tonight so be off by six." As Katherine came around the desk and gave him a kiss he then replied "I guess I'll see you at six."

While Katherine exited from out of the office Brad then sent a text message to Fallon's phone telling her that if she wanted the home, she got it and to meet him back at the office that night. As Fallon taken a look at the message and smiled, she then went to shop for something suitable to wear. Something that would complement her figure and to keep him distracted so he wouldn't think of changing his mind. As the night set in and Fallon was on her way Brad made sure that he was able to set the mood right by ordering a platter of fruit and wine, to entertain his guest. Once Fallon walked in and seen that the place was lit up with candles she then replied "oh my, let me guess you must do this for all your guest." As he rushed over to her with a wine glass and a bottle of wine, he welcomed her in and poured her up a drink and asked if she could sit. Once she taking a seat and started to sip from the glass he then stops her and has her raise her glass for a toast.

As Brad made her raise her glass he then replied "this is to making history now that The Berkley Estates has a new owner." As they clinked their glasses together and took a hefty swallow. He then stared at her for a good ten seconds wondering why she wanted the property and why to be sold as a commercial site. As Fallon thought about what he said she then replied "it's for my own protection, their protection; so they won't say that my business is in illegal use." "Ok that explains so much but if you don't mind me asking, what type of business are you trying to run where you feel the need to feel secured usually the state don't care about you conducting business out of your home." As Fallon looked over at Brad she then laughed and said "come on now if I tell you I'm sure you would be the first to judge me out of all." Brad replies, "judging others is not the field I play well in you can tell me anything; but that's only if you're comfortable", as she crossed her legs and finished off her glass of wine. She then replied back to him while lighting a cigarette saying "I'm just trying to build a legacy and by the way if you want to know more you will have to chase it.

Chapter 3. New Paint

Standing in the center of the great room stood Fallon giving orders on where she would like certain items to be placed throughout the home. As the offer between her and Mr. Watson seemed to have worked out in her favor. She was now ready for her big break out into a successful business owner where she would proudly wear the name madam. As Fallon have taking a look around the home and noticed that everything looked fantastic, she then walked out on to the front porch to get some fresh air. While she stood looking out into the streets, she then cracked a smile and chuckled to herself as she knew that she has gotten what she wanted. Once she has turned back around to head back into the home, she then noticed the dry and chipped paint that was peeling from the exterior of the home. As she taking a look at the damages and rubbed her fingers across the paint, she then walked down the steps of the home and noticed that the front could use a touch up.

When she realized that the front needed a new appearance, she wasted no time coming up with an idea, as she went to grab a ladder and a container of paint. When Fallon placed the ladder in place and opened the container of paint, she said unto herself "well, well, well looks like I chose correctly, a girl can never go wrong with the color pink." Once she settled on using the paint that she has magically chosen she then painted over the spots that were bruised and continued to paint to give the home a newer look. While she painted away at the home there was a woman that stood on the opposite side of the gate watching her as she went over every spot. As the woman watched on, she then caught her attention by clearing her throat and replying "nice touch" once the woman spoke Fallon became nervous and dropped the brush. As the brush fell to the ground and Fallon climbed down to retrieve it, the woman then apologized "I am so sorry I did not mean to scare you", Fallon replies "you sure because I was very focus on what I was doing and didn't realize you was standing there.

"I am so positive" said the woman, as Fallon turned her back and walked back towards the ladder. The woman then shouted over the gate "so you're the new owner", Fallon responds "yeah." As the woman took a look at the house she then smirked at Fallon and told her that she loved what she has done with the place. As Fallon thanked her for her compliment and went back to repainting, the woman then said "Juanita would be proud of you." As Fallon caught on to the name that the woman spoke of. She quickly came down from off the ladder and stood foot in the grass and replied "Juanita! What do you know about Juanita? As the woman came walking around the gate into the yard to get closer to her, she then replied "who doesn't know Juanita, Ms. Juanita was one of the greatest madams this city could ever have; she was well known uptown and south of the tracks, people use to refer her as the woman with plenty." As Fallon stood wondering why, she was the woman with plenty. The woman then told her that it was a nickname to say she was the woman that brought plenty of pussy to the table. As the woman stood reminiscing the good times of Juanita, she also brought up the struggle. "Juanita ran one of the best underground brothel homes until one night the feds came breaking down doors and windows just to arrest her and her girls, they didn't find any drugs nor have a search warrant to search the home; rumor has it to this day that it had something to do with race and that crooked conservative committee leader the history of this house is tragic to bad that her legacy couldn't live on."

As Fallon thought about what the woman was explaining to her and thought about the legacy of Juanita not being celebrated. Fallon then thought that it was the perfect time to tell her about the home. "I've read the stories on Ms. Juanita, and I can say that it was a very interesting piece; so interesting that it made me want to purchase this home." Before Fallon was able to say anything else the woman cut her off and replied "and now your living in it just like any other would just to say they did it." Fallon responded quickly "actually that is where you are wrong, I don't live here I work here", as the woman looked passed Fallon and scoped out the house. She then replied "so what you are saying is that this is now a business and not some funky museum or a house they just wanted to sale to make a quick buck." Fallon sighs as she knew that it was Brads plan to do exactly what the woman said they were going to do "what I'm telling you is that you're looking at today's madam because I done restored The Berkley Estates; you are looking at the new and improved 52nd Berkley and woodbine brothel, an as of now I'm just looking for some girls to fill this bitch and we can have this thing jumping in no time."

As the woman stood silently popping her gum and looking at her up and down, she then said "you need some then I know some." As the woman went down into her purse and took out a business card and handed it off to her. She then encouraged Fallon to come see her perform and then after she could meet the ladies. While Fallon grabbed ahold of the card and took a look at it, she then replied "I'll definitely be there thank you." As the woman walked off from Fallon she then came to a pause and replied with a smirk on her face "you better and by the way the name is Kardea, and you welcome. As Kardea left from the brothel home Fallon then headed back up the steps and into the home. As she stood in the center of the great room and viewed how everything magically came together, suddenly there was a knock at the door. As Fallon went to answer the door there was Brad standing with a bouquet of flowers in his hand and a card that has been wrapped and sealed.

As she wondered who the flowers were for Brad then placed them in her arms and congratulated her "lovely lady these are for you." As Fallon held on to the flowers and welcomed him in, she then thanked him and mentioned how beautiful they were "these are so beautiful." Brad replies "Well, I am glad that you like them I handpicked them just for you down at Lilys flowerpot off of Langston. "Are you serious?" asked Fallon "I am so serious" said Brad, Fallon starts to become overwhelmed "you didn't have to do that," said Fallon. As Brad agreed with her, he then mentioned to her how he couldn't help but to "but I needed to, this is your moment, and this is my congratulations to you." As Fallon thanked him for his sweet gesture, she then found a place to sit the flowers. As she sat the flowers in a vase on a mantel above the fireplace. She then turned back around to Brad and smiled saying "it looks nice huh", Brad nods his head as he said "yes."

While both stood in the middle of the great room gazing at the flowers and at each other. Fallon then offered to give him a tour of the home, as Brad agreed to the offer. He then followed behind her complimenting the home every step of the way as he fell in love with her sense of style. "You know what you really have a sense of style; I just really love what you have done with the place," said Brad. Fallon replied "well if it wasn't for you taking a chance on renovating; I don't think I would have been this determined or have any clue on where to start." As Brad took her by her two hands he responded "no don't say that about yourself, you knew exactly how to get started." As Brad happened to notice the time on his watch he then replied "well, well, well look at the time, I might as well get going; I know they are expecting me down at the office anytime soon now." Fallon recommended "Then you might want to get a move on then", Before Brad decided to let go of her hands he then replied "you know it's funny how time fly's when you are having fun." As Fallon begins to burst into a slight chuckle he then replied in laughter "what what's so funny", Fallon replies "really Brad Janet" "hey it made you smile didn't it" said Brad "I guess it may have," said Fallon.

As Brad became quiet and stood face to face with Fallon, Fallon then wondered what could possibly be on his mind. "Whoa' Brad are you ok; you went silent on me there" said Fallon, as she placed her hand upon his shoulder and begun to rub it. He then replied in a low tone as he starts to experience some guilt "you know sometimes I wonder why I even do the things I do, why I'm even in the career that I'm in, why I even make this decision knowing that my wife is going to kill me." As Fallon looked up into his eyes and smirked, she then replied "it's because you are the man and sometimes being the man comes with making stressful decisions that doesn't always accommodate everyone's needs and desires; trust me I get it soon that would be me, it's all about being a boss." "You know that really made sense; you really have a way with words," said Brad. Fallon replies, "well is that so?" "Hell yea" Brad responded. While Fallon and Brad both laughed amongst each other Fallon then thought about Brad mentioning his wife wondering what was her look on him selling the property. "So, your wife what was her thoughts on you making a big sale?" said Fallon. Brad shakes his head "she doesn't know, and I plan to keep it that way," said Brad. As Brad took a deep breath, he then replied "sometimes business and relationships doesn't always work well together", "isn't that the truth" replied Fallon.

As Fallon wondered what she did for a living, Brad then told her about her leadership roll over the woman conservative committee. Claiming it to be a pain in his ass a major headache and wished that it would be sabotaged. "So, your wife is a conservative republican?" asked Fallon, "that she is and one of the main reasons she doesn't know about this property being sold is because she would do anything in her will power to try and take it down especially if she finds out that it's back to being a Brothel" said Brad. As Fallon twisted up her face at him' as she couldn't believe all that she was hearing, she then decided to ask Brad why he decided to acknowledge her decision "so why did you consider my decision although your wife thinks differently." As Brad stepped in close to her and grabbed a hold of her chin while looking into her eyes he then replied with "sometimes the devil has to have a place to play while also having a place to lay."

While Fallon kept her eyes glued to him as he kept her chin tilted upward, she then said to him "and where the devil lays there will always be a couple of strays with a price to pay." While Brad continued to look into Fallon's eyes he then replied "sometimes a man has to get free to be at peace." Once Brad let go of Fallon's chin and Fallon continued to stare into his ocean blue eyes and rub her fingers through his sandy blonde hair. He then tilted her chin back up and begun to kiss her, as he delivered a kiss to her lips. She then wrapped her arms around his neck and started to kiss him back, allowing him to feel the warm tender sensation of her lips pressed up against his. While he took both of his hands and applied it to her waistline, he then backed her onto a bean bag that sat on the left hand side of her desk and begun to kiss all over her neck. As Fallon became horny for him and wanted his body pressed against hers, she then begun to undress him while she made him undress her from the waist down. Once Brad pulled down her panties and crumbled them into the palms of his hands from getting a good whiff of them. He then started to suck and squeeze on her boobs while reaching over for a rubber from out of his wallet in his pants pocket. Once Fallon laid back caressing her boobs and Brad managed to put the condom on. There he was inserting his dick into her as he moaned, groaned and sweated while applying pressure "oh fuck, ahh fuck."

~The Pink Pony~

As night has fallen and The Pink Pony's girls were off to a good start entertaining the fellas. People begun to show up and show out as cars flooded the parking lots and streets. To many folks in town The Pink Pony was the place to be if you were looking for one of the most top notched lap dances or a thrilled sexual experience away from home.

Rumor has it that most men that look forward to attending The Pink Pony have either just got into an argument with their woman or their dicks are too stiff for it to stroke itself. As the ballers posted up center stage making it rain and girls came crashing down the poles into splits and tricks. You just knew that the club was going to be lit. As Fallon made her way through security into the club and stood looking at the crowd become wild up from all the attention they were receiving. She then made her way to a corner that sat and empty table and took a seat to watch the performance. While she sat to herself looking sexy in an all-black cat suit and dazzling golden pumps. Called on to the stage was no other then Kardea dripping in silver and diamonds as she hit the stage in a blinged out corset and bottoms with a cowgirl hat to match.

While Fallon sat back in her chair enjoying the view of Kardea tossing her ass in a circle. You can say that she was impressed by the skills that she was delivering. As Kardea magically worked the pole for a full 20 minutes, her skills showed that she was that bitch and that she was built to be that girl that never dealt with a competition. While she mastered the pole as good as she did Fallon was left speechless as she cheered and applauded her after her set. As Fallon sat to herself with two shots placed on the table. Down came Kardea walking over towards the table in so much excitement to see her. As Fallon stood up from her seat and applauded her. Kardea became ecstatic as she was happy that she enjoyed the show "I see that somebody enjoyed the show", "enjoyed are you serious I fucking loved it you killed that shit," said Fallon. As Fallon stood looking at Kardea she replied "bitch you amaze me, I don't even think I would have what it takes to even do half of the tricks you done." Kardea chuckles "girl that's why you practice; now I can't speak on any other hoe in here, but you best believe I gives it my all."

While Fallon and Kardea took a seat down at the round table Fallon then wanted to know about the girls she supposed to be bringing to her. "So how about these girls, are they ready to meet their new boss," said Fallon. Kardea laughs "girl what new girls?", "I thought you was going to have some new girls waiting for me!" said Fallon. As Kardea flips back her hair and folds her arms she responded "look around does it look like any of these hoes are ready to leave? This is home to them this is where they make their money, they not about to give up scrubbing the ground to come submit to sucking ten niggas dicks, blowjobs are like charity." "Did you even talk to them about it?" said Fallon, Kardea replies, why should I talk to these hoes about it, if I'm the only bitch that would consider to get the job done. Fallon throws up her hands in disappointment before noticing what Kardea said "Kardea are you serious! Wait, wait a minute did you just say?" Kardea responds "see you doing all that talking but not enough listening, I said I'm down." As Fallon sat up straight in her chair and took a sip of the glass water that sat beside her shot of Patron. She then replied "great but what will you do about here?", Kardea replied "it seems like the pink pony is just going to have to miss me for a while, these streets is tough and I got to blow money fast out this bitch." As Fallon handed over the shot of Patron to Kardea, Fallon and Kardea both raised their glasses as they toasted to her successful night and to her being the first Babe of Ladies nights "business is now open."

Chapter 4. The Grand Opening

Now that the Brothel house done got some new paint, Fallon was off to a great start with her lead lady Kardea. Now that the Brothel house was gearing up for business things were starting to heat up. As Fallon done ushered in some new girls and one of Kardea closest friends from The Pink Pony. Sapphire was also well known as one of The Pink Pony's main pole masters. She was ruthless, risky and full of personality, just that type of girl that believed in turning a sour night into a good night. Down at The Pink Pony a lot of the men crowned her the nickname Knockout, rumor has it that when she bounces that ass, she lays nigga's to sleep. While all of the girls were standing around and talking amongst each other in the great room. In came the head bitch in charge herself Ms. Fallon demanding everyone to line up and to face her. As every one of the girls followed her instructions and lined up in a straight line, she then pulled Kardea out from the line and told her to stand by her.

While Kardea did just that Fallon then stood front and center and made the big announcement "ok ladies showtime is around the corner but first may I welcome all of you to the all-new and improved Brothel house of 52nd Berkley and woodbine, Ladies welcome to Ladies nights." As the women of the brothel cheered in excitement by applauding the launch of Ladies nights, Fallon then went over some rules to make sure that the women were caught up to speed. Rule #1. "No finessing", Rule #2. "No freebies" Rule #3. "If he doesn't have the funds to make him cum, no fuck", Rule #4. "No link ups", Rule #5. "No drug use", Rule #6. "Protect your stack", Rule #7. "Avoid pigs", Rule #8. "Leave at appropriate time", Rule #9. "Have fun" and Rule #10. "Obey your Madam and security." Once Fallon done laid down the rules of the home, she then turned to Kardea and told her that now the floor was hers.

As Fallon walked over to her desk and begun to shuffle through some papers, Kardea followed behind her and replied "I understand that I'm your leading lady and all but what the fuck you think I suppose to do with these heffas; I can't teach these hoes how to swallow up a dick and tickle a niggas nut sacks." Fallon drops the stack of papers on to the desk as she laughs out loud "girl I'm serious" said Kardea. Fallon responds, "you may not know how to teach these girls how to give sloppy toppy; but one thing for sure that I know, is that you could teach them how to have rhythm." Kardea folds up her arms and replied "how's that possible when you don't even have a pole insight." Fallon steps to Kardea and whispered "never say never because anything is possible", as Fallon picked up her purse and headed towards the door Kardea shouts "where are you going, you not going to stay around for the show?" Fallon turns towards Kardea and the girls and said "to lunch a bitch is hungry and by the way if you hoes want to eat, the fridge and cabinets in the kitchen are packed with all types of good stuff have at it." As Fallon headed out the door to grab her some French chowder. Kardea then turned to the girls and replied "before you heffas even think of a sandwich or a soda pop we got some work to do, now fall in line."

~boarded motel~

As the girls was left, at the house to learn how to provide customer satisfaction skills, there was one girl that hustled in her own way to make ends meet while also looking for a great escape. (Women's voice) "ah, ah, right there", (male voice) "ah oh yes baby your such a fucking angel; I'm about to nut keep going." (woman's voice)" ah yes papi you like that pussy" males eyes roll back in his head as he grunts "ugh ahh, ahh, ahh", as the woman removes herself from on top of him, he then begins to remove the sweat from off his forehead with a hand towel. As she rolls over on the side of him and sticks her hand out, the man begun to laugh and say that she was tripping. As she became frustrated with him, she then yelled "stop with the games and hand over the money", As the man pulls up his pants and reaches down into his pockets. He then pulls out some cash and throws it in front of her on to the bed "there's your cut", as she reached for the money and begun to count, she then shouted "you must be joking, Pablo said 200 this is only $80 where's the rest of it."

As the man reached back down into his pockets and pulled his pockets inside out he then replied "umm I guess I don't got it, but look if you tell Pablo to pay me back I swear I'll put the money in your hands", the woman yells in rage "you have to be fucking kidding me do you know what Pablo would do to me if I don't have his money?" "Look trick that's not my problem; tell Pablo to book better rooms instead of cheap ass motels and maybe the princess could be taking care of better," shouted the man. As she grabbed ahold of her purse and stashed the money at the bottom of the bag, she then made her way towards the door and headed down the steps of the motel. As the man continued to shout from the top of the staircase, she then kept to herself as she thought of what to say when she arrives back home.

Once she made it back home, she entered the home in silence as she did not want Pablo to hear her coming in. As she managed to walk slowly throughout the home to get to the bathroom to take a shower. She came across a loose floor board that creaked loudly as she stepped on top of it. While stepping on the loose floor board brought fear to her heart, she then took a deep breath and continued to walk towards the bathroom. As she kept looking straight ahead while passing an entry way to the living room that she dared not to look in. There was Pablo sitting in the middle of the room with the television on mute calling her name, as Miracle stood still when he called her name. She then turned back around and walked in the living room to see what he needed from her. As Miracle stood at the doorway of the room, he then told her to move in a little closer "you could get a little closer than that, you know I like you front and center," said Pablo. As Miracle moved in closer to him and took a stand in the middle of the room. Pablo then asked her about her time with the john "so how did it go?", Miracle responds in a low tone "It went good sir", "cool let me hold the cash," said Pablo.

As Miracle reached down in her purse and handed over the cash shaking, nervously, Pablo begins to question her "you alright mommy you shaking." Miracle nods her head as she replies, "yes daddy I'm ok", as Pablo begun counting the cash and noticed that the money was short. He then begun to question her "I know that you can count you are a smart girl, but this is only 80 bucks where the fuck is the rest of it." Miracle sighs as she tried to explain herself "I don't know", Pablo becomes angry and begins to shout "what the fuck you mean you don't know". As Miracle stood shrugging her shoulders, Pablo then shouted "go get my money, go get my fucking money right now." Miracle shouts "I can't", "what the fuck you mean you can't you suppose to been fucked for 200 not $80," said Pablo. As Pablo stood to his feet in a hurry and grabbed ahold of her arm. He then begun to shake her while placing fear into her as he screamed off the top of his lungs for her to get his money. As Miracle told him that she couldn't she then explained to him why "I'm sorry but I didn't know that this was going to happen, after the fuck I told Dominic to pay me but he refused to pay the full 200; he told me he didn't have it and that when you pay him back he would let me hold." As Pablo squeezed her arm and looked into her eyes, he then replied "pay him! pay him back I don't owe him shit, mommy you been finessed this motherfucker played you; and when a motherfucker plays you that means they played me."

While Miracle stood in tears apologizing with her arm being held by Pablo, Pablo then looks at her and tells her to strip. As Miracle stood looking up at him and shaking her head no. Pablo then yells loudly "strippp" and back hand slaps her across the face." As Miracle fell to the floor holding her face and trying to crawl away from him. He then walked up to her and kicks her in the stomach saying "you know you make it so hard for me to fucking love you, now get up, get the fuck up now." As Pablo grabbed ahold of her hair and pulled her up from the floor he then whispered in her ear "you're going to do what I say and give me what I want" while stripping her out of her skirt and panties." As Pablo placed his hand over her mouth with his arm wrapped around her waist, he then forces her into the bedroom and throws her on the bed while delivering a spank to the right side of her ass cheek. While she gripped on to the other side of the bed and tried to pull herself up Pablo then climbed on the back of her and thrusted his penis up against her ass while holding down her hand. As he whispered in her ear to not move and to feel him, Miracle then back headbutted him in the face and turned and delivered a kick with both of her two feet knocking him down into the corner of the bed. As she quickly got up from the bed and ran down the hall she quickly grabbed ahold of her skirt and purse and made a run for it out of the home.

As Miracle ran with the hopes of no looking back, she quickly took shelter at a seafood diner on the boulevard. As she took a seat in the far-left corner of the diner away from the windows, she then placed her head upon the table so she wouldn't be seen if Pablo came looking for her. As Fallon entered the diner and walked up to the counter, to grab ahold of her chowder that she has ordered. She then decided that she would take a seat and enjoy her lunch inside of the diner instead of the house. While she dived into her French fish chowder enjoying every bite of it, she then happens to look over at Miracle as Miracle tried to fix her make up. As Miracle tried fixing her make up by adding extra blush and foundation around her eye and her jaw, Fallon then walked over to the table and offered her, her foundation kit as she seen Miracle was becoming frustrated. As Miracle looked up at her and thanked her for the makeup, Fallon then asked if she could sit with her. As Miracle seemed unsure and nervous about Pablo spotting her out, Fallon then told her that she has nothing to worry about because one bullet from her pistol would take him out indefinitely.

While Fallon sat staring at Miracle, Miracle then started to cry as she cried out "I suppose to be dead, I swear I suppose to be dead why am I here?" Fallon responds to Miracle "maybe it's because it's not your time to go, if the man upstairs wanted you to go due to the hands of that motherfucker, he would of allowed it but that's not the way he has planned for you to go." As Miracle takes Fallon by her hands, she then replied "he beats me, says he loves me, sells me to make money for himself and when he doesn't get his way or becomes frustrated about anything he holds me down and takes it out on my pussy." As Fallon shed a tear listening to Miracle speak about her physical abusive relationship with her boyfriend she then replied, "you don't have to go through this anymore", as Miracle shrugged her shoulder's and confessed that she doesn't know what she's going to do. Fallon then recommended her to run to never look back and to start over, as Miracle continued to shrug her shoulders. She then replied, "look at me I'm a prostitute with no money, no car, no extra hustle all I have is these marks that I keep allowing Pablo to place upon my body I'm so stupid." "Stupid no, naïve and scared yes, us women get that way sometimes when we feel less than what our worth says we are," said Fallon. As a waiter came over to check on Fallon to see how she was enjoying her food, Fallon then told them that the food was excellent and to make a second one to go for her friend sitting across from her.

As Miracle told Fallon that she didn't have to, Fallon then insisted that she must. While Fallon sat waiting for the chowder to be prepared, she then asked Miracle if she was ok with a place to stay for tonight and tomorrow. As Miracle shook her head yes and wondered why, Fallon then reached down into her purse and pulled out a card to Ladies Nights with some cash. "Here take it, if you don't find anywhere else to go after these two days feel free to come to this address, I'll have a bed and a room ready for you." As Miracle looked down at the card and replied, "what's Ladies Nights?", Fallon then responded, "a place where a sisterhood is built, money is to be made and a place to call home." As Miracle sat and thought about what she was saying, Fallon then passed her the cup a French chowder and told her to eat. Once Fallon rose from her seat and placed her purse upon her shoulder she then replied, "I would love to stay and chat with you until the stars come out; but I got to tend to these girls they have a big night tomorrow night, so I have to run." As Fallon walked off from the table Miracle then grabbed her attention as she asked, "what's tomorrow night", Fallon smirks as she turns around and says, "it's grand opening time."

~Grand opening at Ladies Nights~

While Fallon returned to the brothel home from her lunch, the ladies remained hyped about the grand opening and was excited to show off their new moves. Thanks to Kardea she was able to break them in to delivering some sexy dance moves to go along with them seducing their clients. As Fallon done placed her purse down on to the desk and taking a seat. Kardea noticed that she seemed a little down about something "boss lady you ok, now earlier you walked out of here feeling mighty fine; now you come back, and you look like you been run over by a truck." Fallon looks up at Kardea and replied, I'm so glad you have a heart, but I am ok I just feel a little sleepy." "Well, you better wake up grandma because you got work to do because your lady to teach this class should be here in any minute now" said Kardea. As there was a knock at the door Kardea and Fallon both looked at one another and smirked while saying "this shall be fun."

As Fallon went to open up the door of the home for the guest, in came the lady of all sexual tricks to please a man. As the women of the brothel home looked over to see who she was. Sapphire in excitement filled them in on who the woman was and why she was there saying "girl yall don't know who that is, that is the grapefruit lady we are about to learn how to grapefruit a dick today bitches." As the woman stepped further into the home and said hello to everyone, Fallon then filled the ladies in on who she was. "Ladies I would like you to meet Amber Riley she is the grapefruit expert, she's about to make sure that yall are taught how to be a dick sucking expert with fruit before the grand opening." "So, all eyes on her because you may need to bust out a few tricks to wild that niggah's dreams, if he pays for it" said Kardea, "grapefruit queen the floor is yours and Ladies Nights it's your time to shine," said Fallon.

While the babes of the brothel home learned how to be more provocative and learned a sweet new technique, you could say that they were ready for grand opening. As the doors to Ladies Nights were open the men rolled in like it was stripper bowl Friday at a strip club, thanks to Kardea and Sapphire causing a buzz on social media. As the girls were snatching up men one by one and fulfilling their wildest fantasies, money floated in quicker than Fallon has ever thought. As Kardea came walking down the hall to the great room all that the men could do was stare at her ass and talk about how bad they would love to climb in it. As Kardea came over to Fallon she then replied, "I can get use to this, the paper is coming in quick and these horny niggas just can't get enough, grand opening is lit sis." Fallon chuckles "girl you can say that again, we rolling in stacks tonight", as Fallon and Kardea stood talking amongst one another they noticed that the men that were standing in line were hyped up about that seemed out of the ordinary. Once Fallon and Kardea heard a commotion they both ran towards the sight and found security choking up a dude that tried to force himself upon one of the girls.

As Fallon told the men that were in line to make way, she then ordered security to throw him outside. Once security got the memo, they then picked up the man and tossed him on to the front porch. As the man became upset and tried to come back inside the home, Fallon then walked over to the door and blocked his entrance saying "you know you remind me of someone who I read about, he didn't commit the same crime as you; but he did disobey mothers' rules and tried to fight his way back in." As the man shouted at Fallon telling her to let him back in and that he was going to kick one of the babes ass. Fallon then walks up to him and tells him to calm down while delivering a backhand slap to his face and telling him to get the fuck off her steps. While the man fled the home, and she came walking back in, she then told the other guys that if they ever think of pulling the same stunt that they would receive the same punishment. While Fallon stood back in her corner cooling off from her feud, Kardea then replied, "damn I see you boss lady you handle your shit", Fallon laughs as she responds with "the bitch had it coming."

While Fallon stood checking in the men to be seen by the babes, Kardea then tapped her on the shoulder and said "girl who is that white man over there and why is he grilling you so hard." As Fallon takes a look at who Kardea is speaking of, her mouth then dropped as she seen that it was Mr. Watson. As Fallon told Kardea to take over the guest check in's and excused herself from the great room. She then walked over to brad and said "Brad wow I wasn't expecting you to be here what a surprise." As Brad stood smiling at her he then replied, "I saw the add and the post online and I thought that I would come and surprise you", "well I am very surprised," said Fallon. "Well like I said before sometimes the devil has to have somewhere to play; while also having somewhere to lay" said

Brad, "so you came to be a bad boy?" said Fallon. As Brad pulls her into his arms, he then said to her "yes madam now come up stairs to your throne I have something to show you." Once Brad welcomed her up to the master suite, she then looked behind her at the crowd and Kardea.

Once she seen that Kardea was getting the men in and out and that security were on their shit. She wasted no time taking Brad by the hand while heading up the steps. As they made it upstairs to the master in the center of the floor sat a cage, as Fallon taking a look at the cage she then replied, "oh I see what this is your brought me up here for some freak shit; motherfucker is that a dog cage in the middle of my floor." Brad grabs her by the waist and brings her in closer "calm down baby it's not an actual dog cage; this is more of a dog cage made for humans for sexual foreplay." Fallon cuts her eye at the cage and back at brad and replied, "well damn I see that times has really changed in the world of toys." As Brad lifted her chin and stared into her eyes he then replied, "that it has and with this cage I want my wildest fantasies to be met; I want to test it out with you."

While Fallon moved his hand from her chin and kissed his lips while rubbing a finger down his chest she then replied, "you know you really are some types of freak white boy." As Fallon walked over to the cage and opened the door to crawl in, she then turns around and finds Brad fully naked with a muzzle to put over his mouth. As Fallon was curious of what he was trying to do Brad then walked over to her and said, "when I purchased this cage, I didn't purchase it for you to crawl inside, it happens to be for me." As the look upon Fallon's face showed she was in complete shock, Brad then got down on his knees and begun to crawl into the cage. Once he was down on all fours inside of the cage with the door locked and a hole for inserting. He then said to Fallon "they say you're not a real man until you get your ass ate; I figure tonight I'll become that man by having my groceries ate, madam can you make me into a real man." As Fallon looked at his sexy posture and seen how he was willing and ready. She then told him to put the muzzle on and to shut up, as she walked around and examined his ass. Once she made it to the back of him and felt on both of his cheeks, he then replied, "madam I'm sorry to disturb you but I also have some dildos that you can use to have fun on me." As Fallon told him to put the muzzle back on and spanked his cheeks, she grabbed a hold of his ass and sucked the middle as he moaned "oh yes right there oh yes eat me madam."

Chapter 5. Fly High

As the days have went by and grand opening was a big success for the ladies down at Ladies nights, Ladies nights have now become the talk of the city. One of the biggest talks in the city to land in the paper, radio and even on social media, gaining exposure to the business. As majority of everyone in the city were proud of the new establishment. There was one person that thought highly different about the business and couldn't stand to look or hear about it. Entering the office of Brad Watson and slamming down a newspaper on to his desk, was no other than Katherine Watson "what's this can you please explain to me what the hell I am looking at," shouted Katherine. Brad places his hands over his face while saying "I just knew there would be no hiding this from you", Katherine shouts "your damn right about that; like are you kidding me, Brad." Brad quickly stood up from his chair and replied, "it was a good investment, ok", as Katherine mocks Brad and calls him an idiot she then replied "what's so good about selling a half a million dollar home to a party animal; please enlighten me."

While Mrs. Watson shown that she was highly upset with her husband, Brad then took a seat upon the edge of his desk and said, "look I know to you this may seem like a mistake, but this actually helped out the company and myself." As Katherine begun to laugh and roll her eyes at him, she then replied, "how funny that you mention yourself, what about me where was my cut in this deal." As Brad sat quietly thinking about how she never wanted the deal to go through he then responded, "what are you talking about you never wanted a cut because you were against it." Katherine shouted "exactly, your right I was against it, and I still am I just find it selfish that you couldn't place your pride to the side to do the right thing for this family and that was to never sell." As Brad stood up from his desk with his finger pointing to her face, he then shouted off the top of his lungs "you're going to stop telling me what to do, I call the shots this is my company not yours." As Katherine stood with one of her hands over her chest, as she couldn't believe that he would scream at her.

She then looked down at the paper and mentioned how her mother would be so disappointed if she was to find out about the Berkley Estates being sold off. As Brad shrugged his shoulders and went back to working on another sale. Katherine then shook her head and replied "how despicable what is Ladies Nights and look how all of them are dressed; this is exactly why me and my team push awareness amongst the community so little girls won't turn out to be like that." As Brad lit a cigarette and placed it to his mouth he then replied, "honey is you done?", as Katherine looked over at him, she then replied "oh I'm more than just done I'm just getting started." As Katherine snatched the paper from off his desk and slammed the door behind her, she then headed back up to her office and tossed the newspaper at the wall. As Ms. Watson sat to herself at her desk furious that the Berkley Estates was sold off, she then thought of an idea that would leave Brad disappointed.

As for the women back at the brothel there was no telling them that they were disappointed, as conversations about the grand opening came up more than once throughout the home. While Fallon made her way down to the main floor and headed into the kitchen, there were the other women sitting around the table chatting it up over some, breakfast. As Fallon stopped in between the doorway and looked at the girls socialize amongst each other she then replied, "now this is what I like to see, good morning, ladies." "Good morning boss lady" said the other women, as

Fallon headed over to the fridge to grab something to drink. In came Kardea grabbing her attention "I'm going to need you to put that back boss lady", "and why is that?" wondered Fallon. "Maybe because there's already a plate and a cup of OJ prepared for you" said Kardea. While Fallon took a look around the table at the delicious breakfast that was prepared, she then spotted out a plate of egg scrambled, toast and bacon. That was left at the foot of the table with a tall glass of orange juice just for her. When Fallon seen the plate, she quickly rushed over to the table and took a seat telling the girls how she appreciates the sweet gesture, and they deserve nothing but the best.

While Fallon sat diving into her breakfast, she then looked around the table at the girls and said, "so I see that the night of grand opening got a bitch not wanting to go home." Sapphire replies "girl, grand opening was lit, I was able to bring in a couple of stacks without even having to rely on another night." Fallon chuckles at Sapphire as she replied, "well, I'm glad that you enjoyed yourself and looked sexy while doing it in all of that melanin", Kardea responds "suit yourself." As Fallon turned and cut her eye at her, she then responded "girl hush" while providing a slight chuckle, "seems like grand opening got you not wanting to go home as well from the little night you had" said Kardea. As everyone at the table was trying to figure out what Kardea was talking about, Kardea then revealed that Fallon took a white man up to her suite. As the girls at the table giggled and was excited to know all about it, Fallon then looked over at Kardea with a smirk and replied, "oh baby it was good, quite interesting but sexy and let's just say he do know how to throw that dick."

As the girls laughed and cheered her on Fallon then replied, "he's quite a freak, maybe Ms. Kardea should snag her one let him break her off a little of that ahh what she calls it' pink meat", "girl you want some pink meat" shouted out Sapphire. As Kardea stood in tears from laughing and all the girls just giggled away suddenly there was a knock at the door. As the girls became silent as they heard the knock and footsteps of someone on the porch, Fallon then rose from the chair and headed over to see who it could be. Once Fallon opened the door and saw that it was Miracle, she then allowed her to come in and sit her belongings to the side of the door. While Fallon looked at Miracle she then replied, "I guess you decided to take me up on my offer", as Miracle scoped out the room she then said in a low tone "I didn't have anywhere else to go." "Well now you do come on and get your stuff" said Fallon, While Fallon was showing Miracle to her room, off in the distance stood Kardea and Sapphire.

While they watched Fallon go over the rules of the home and told her to make herself at home. Kardea then became furious as she steps to Fallon and said "wait a minute who is she?" Fallon looks Kardea up and down and replies "excuse me nosey but if you shall know this here is Miracle, she's our new edition to the brothel' she's going to be a babe." As Kardea eyeballed Miracle and looked back at Fallon she then replied, "so I guess home gurl just get to slide on through without any practice huh?" Fallon sighs "now Kardea what does that supposed to mean", Kardea replies, "that she thinks she can just walk up in here and have it easy." Miracle responds to Kardea "have it easy really' I didn't even ask to be here", As Kardea stepped to Miracle, she then questioned her "then why are you here?" As Fallon jumps in between Kardea and Miracle she then yelled "ok look that's enough, I understand you want to be the mean girl all the time; but sometimes all of that attitude is just uncalled for, now can you and the girls go back to what you guys were doing in let her be."

As Kardea looked at Miracle then back at Fallon she then replied in a harsh tone "fine but you got some explaining to do on why this hoe gets her own room", "Right because I'm still living with homeboy that comes and tips me at the club," said Sapphire. Fallon snaps "and who's fault is that please allow me to know Sapphire; you know what I just learned something today, that even though yall may be caring yall bitches also can be ungrateful; now allow her to unpack as I excuse myself from you guys." While Fallon have excused herself from the ladies and Miracle started to unpack her belongings, Kardea then approached her while saying "yea go ahead and get a good look at them walls because I'm sure your ass isn't going to be here for that long so you might as well not unpack." As Miracle turned towards Kardea and stepped to her face. She then replied "you know you are such a bully like what is your problem with me? you don't even know me." As Kardea rolled her neck with her hands upon her hips she then said "let's just say I know a hoe when I see one", Miracle responds "I guess that makes all us a hoe since all of us laid on our backs at some time."

While Kardea chuckled at Miracles response she then replied, "bitch at no point did I ever prostituted as a hustle; this bitch strips and pretty damn good at it to, maybe you can talk shit once you headline next to a professional like myself." As Miracle begun to laugh at Kardea, Kardea then questioned her on what was so funny. Miracle responds, "hmm let me guess you must have worked at the pink pony; and if so, I feel bad for you with the sorry reputations you guys have floating around, I can imagine that the only thing you were headlining was giving throat jobs in the back of the club while the other niggas that come to tip you felt bad for you." As Miracle placed her hands upon her hips and rolled her neck back at her, she then replied, "now who's doing the neck rolling." While Kardea stood chuckling underneath her guilt she then struck Miracle with a closed fist and shouted, "hoe, didn't your momma ever tell you to never mock anyone." As Miracle held on to her face and tossed her phone to the side of her, she then rushed towards Kardea and attacked her into the hall. As both of the women were on the floor pulling each other's hair and throwing punches. Down came Fallon breaking up the fight and yelling at Kardea "I thought I told you to leave her alone; what part of leave her alone you don't understand." Kardea looks up at Fallon as she sat on the floor "so you just going to take-up for this trick", as Fallon stood quietly while the other women watched. Kardea then stood to her feet and stormed off into playroom six while Sapphire ran after her.

As Fallon sighed and finally calmed everybody down, she then told everyone to pack their belongings and to head home. Once Fallon begun to give orders to the women of the brothel suddenly there was another knock at the door. As Fallon stormed to the door saying "now who is it" she then opened the door to only find Katherine Watson and the conservative women's committee standing upon the doorstep. As Fallon opened the door she then replied "may I help you", Katherine responds while taking her shades off "my, my, my am I glad to see you", "excuse me but who are you if you don't mind me asking? Asked Fallon. Katherine Watson laughs as she looked side to side and back at her committee "the name is Katherine Watson and these intelligent women that I bring before you are the women of the committee, say hey girls." As the women of the committee waved and said hello, Fallon then replied "it's nice to meet you ladies but we are actually closed but if you'll come back this Tuesday, which is trickster Tuesday I'll be sure to remember your faces."

As Katherine laughed and told her that they weren't there for a show, Miracle then happens to walk up on the side of Fallon and say, "is everything alright boss lady I just unpacked and fixed up my room." While Katherine took one look at Miracle she then shouted, "oh my what a beautiful girl", Fallon replies, isn't she a doll she going to be working with us now; she's our new babe she's been added to the list with all the rest of the girls." Katherine looks at Miracle and replies, "oh really, you know it's just too bad that you're going to waste all that beauty on working in a place like this." Fallon turns to Katherine as she is in shock "wait, wait, wait, wait excuse me come again; I know you just didn't insult one of my girls." Katherine chuckles with the other ladies and replied, "that I did and don't have any regrets for it; Ms. Fallon I expect you to watch your back because me and my girls here, were coming for you and your work of Satan you call a business." Fallon responds, "now you hold up talking to me crazy, to you and your little committee this business may be the work of Satan but to us it's home, it's where we make our money to pay our bills and to the men and women it's where they come to have a good time when there's not any action going on at home."

While Katherine twisted up her face and told the ladies to excuse themselves she then whispered replying " I really don't know what the hell my husband was thinking about when he invested in this property; but one thing for sure is that I will not stand here and watch you and your sex workers parade around here thinking it's ok to fornicate with every Tom, Dick and Harry and give our neighborhood a bad name." Fallon replies "the only person that would be giving this neighborhood a bad name would be yourself up here playing as you a part of the republican party knowing damn well that majority of this neighborhood votes are democratic." As Katherine becomes quiet and places her shades back over her face, she then walked down the porch and turned back to Fallon saying, "you know you're really going to eat your words one day; but as of now the only thing you need to be worried about is watching the money go down the drain, as your business gets voted out of this neighborhood." As Fallon becomes agitated with Mrs. Watson and tells Miracle to get back inside. Mrs. Watson then replied, "my mother would be turning in her grave if she knew that this was going on; but no worries to the both of us because there's a new sheriff in town and this bitch gets things done." As Fallon walked back inside the home and closed the door behind her, off Mrs. Watson and her committee went as they felt as they accomplished a victory.

As Fallon headed up stairs to her suite to think about what just happened, Miracle then headed to her room and closed the door tight behind her. As Kardea was looking out into the hall to see if the halls were clear. She then shut the door of the room her and Sapphire were in and pulled out a snuff tray, as she pulled out the tray and went into her purse to grab the cocaine. Sapphire stood behind her hesitant about her use "Kardea I know that this girl done pissed you off; but do you have to do this right now, you know that drug use is against Fallon's policies." As Kardea lined up the coke on to the tray she then replied "at this point does it look like I give a fuck; seems to me like the bitch is breaking her own rules as of now." Sapphire replies "if this is about that room you can just forget it; I'm sure if we ask if we can have one, she wouldn't mind sparing us a room." While Kardea snorted two lines and turned towards Sapphire she then replied "now bitch you know you could forget about that, you know she just care about the money and that we just here for the ride making it easier for her." As Sapphire stood unclear about how to feel, Kardea then brought the tray up to her and replied "so what's it going to be are you going to talk about Fallon an how she favors this new bitch or you going to fly high off this line with your girl, you pick your poison." While Sapphire stood looking down at the two lines and back up at Kardea she then stomped her two feet and said "what the hell" as she took the pipe and cleared the tray.

Chapter 6. Mocha

As the days went by and Fallon finally got the chance to be to herself without any of the girls. She then headed over to Porters Coffee house to enjoy her a fresh cup of coffee. While she sat pressing her lips against the mug and watching the people walk past, she then called over the waiter to order a strawberry scone with a fresh fruit basket. As she sat with her legs crossed enjoying the view and sipping away at her coffee, in came a fine gentleman that headed towards the front counter to place an order of two chocolate chip muffins and a banana smoothie. While the fine fella bought his breakfast and thanked the barista from behind the counter, he then headed to the outside patio of the diner and went to take a seat at a table that sat by the entrance. While he has taken his seat, he couldn't help but to notice that Fallon was making eye contact with him. As Fallon continued to look away and back at him, he then noticed that they were starting to play a game of eye tag.

Once Fallon looked away and smiled to herself while she sipped her cup of coffee. Standing over her on the opposite side of the table stood the sexy fella asking if he may sit with her. Once Fallon looked up and seen that it was him, she then replied, "I guess why not!", as he took his seat in front of her, he then introduced himself as he stuck his hand out for a handshake "allow me to introduce myself I'm Nathan." As Fallon looked at his hand hanging in midair for a proper greeting, she then reached out for it and gave him a handshake while she introduced herself back to him. As Fallon sat back and sipped her coffee once some more while she sat back smirking at him. He then replied, "so you come to this café often?", Fallon responds "occasionally with my girls but lately it just seems like I never have enough time to do so", Nathen replies, "so today must happen to be that day when you do so." Fallon replied, "that it is but also I just needed to get away and have some time to myself". Nathan chuckles and replies in a low tone "and there is absolutely nothing wrong with that".

As Fallon questioned him on how often he comes to the café he then mentioned that sometimes he visits twice a week. Nathan replied, "I find this to be the best coffee shop here in Detroit, I just love their selection of roasted coffee and I'm also a big fan of their smoke sausage and cheddar biscuit." As Fallon watched him devour his muffin she then laughed and replied, "that isn't the only thing you're a big fan of." "I apologize but these muffins are fire; but off of my muffin what's your favorite item from the menu?" asked Nathan. Fallon replied, "well let's just say I love a good cappuccino, so it would be the vanilla bean machine and as for food I would have to go with the Reuben Club." "Can't forget that dipping sauce" said Nathan, Fallon laughs "oh my gosh yes I love that stuff," said Fallon. As both became quiet and looked into each other's eyes, Nathan then happens to notice that Fallon's clouds in her coffee were starting to fade. As he reached over and grabbed ahold of her cup, he then added some more cream to her coffee and created a swan. "Wow you done that so perfectly" said Fallon, "that's because I use to be a barista," said Nathan. Fallon shouted, "are you serious?", Nathan replies, "dead serious I use to work down at Artistry Coffee House off of Banquet Ave; until I switched my profession and became a police officer."

While Fallon stirred the clouds inside her coffee, she then raised her eyebrow and said, "well that's a great profession although I cannot speak for all." As Fallon called the waiter over for the check, Nathan then asked her "so what do you do for a living Ms. Fallon." Fallon stops mixing the clouds in her coffee and replied in a low tone "something you possibly wouldn't understand; plus, I like to keep my job confidential, but thanks for asking." As Nathan threw up his hands and begun to laugh while sitting back in his chair, he then replied "ooouuu shut down, I take it were playing a little hard to get." As Fallon rose from the table after signing her receipt she then said, "whoever said I was interested?!" Nathan shakes his head as he starts to crack up laughing "damn you with all the shits this morning", "and I'm sure your bowels are saying the same about you; after you done downed that coffee and that muffin that was loaded with nothing but chocolate, I'm sure their stall can use a little company," said Fallon. As Nathan looked up at Fallon with a straight face as she chuckled at her joke towards him, he then replied, "when would I be able to see you again." Fallon sighs and replied, "I'm quite a busy woman but since I see it may be hard to get you away from me here's my number", as Fallon wrote her number on a napkin and slipped it into his shirt while delivering a pat to his chest. She then said her goodbyes and went to exit the patio, as Nathan turned around and watched her walk away he then caught her attention before she exited out of the patio and said "you sure is a comedian, but whatever it is that you do that you feel you need to keep a secret just know that I don't care." As Fallon stood blushing over Nathan, she then told him that she would love to chitchat a little more, but a bitch got some boss bitch shit to tend to.

~Mrs. Watson's Office~

While Fallon was off to being the boss lady that she was, Mrs. Watson was on a new mission to take her down as she sat behind her desk searching through multiple folders for the bill that has been veto. As Watson continued her search, she then became frustrated as the bill wasn't showing up in any of the folders. While she decided to check the last folder that was tucked away in the back of the filing cabinet. She then became even more frustrated as the bill wasn't in that folder neither. As Watson stood looking at the folders on the floor that she done searched through, she then begun to kick the filing cabinet and also slam the doors as she let out a big scream shouting "fuck, fuck, fuck, fuck my life." Once she took a seat at her desk to cool off, in came Grace the receptionist to see if she was ok and to let her know that she has a visitor. As she sat up from her seat and took a sip of water she then responded "visitor what visitor I don't even have any appointments today.

As Grace stood still looking fearful of Mrs. Watson she then replied "did I say visitor I meant to say visitors." While Katherine chugged down her bottle of water, she then closed up her bottle and threw it at Grace and replied "please don't be stupid all your life, do me a favor and let them in." As Grace stood steal in shock, in came Fallon and half of the brothel babes barging into her office. "Well, well, well am I so glad to see you; and what a lovely office you have you must being doing things big; and oh my gosh your receptionist is gorgeous, you know honey it's too bad you're going be wasting them looks working up in here" said Fallon. "What in the hell you think you are doing? Asked Katherine' Fallon steps to her with two hands upon her desk and replied "just returning a favor, me and my girls found your attitude left on our steps and we decided to send it back to you," said Fallon. As Katherine stood up from her chair in such rage, she then asked Fallon "so is this your way of getting revenge; because if so, you just don't know what I have planned for you and your over sexualized entourage." Fallon looks her up and down and replied "maybe so and you can stick, plot and scheme anyway possible and I swear on your mother's grave that we will be ready for them cheap ass stones you throw."

As Katherine came from around her desk and came face to face with Fallon she then replied "I see you like playing with fire; just know that if you don't give up this whore house that you claim you run as a business, I will pull some strings to get the police and detectives involved." While Fallon and the girls burst out into a laughter Fallon then pointed her finger in her face and said "look you owe uppity miserable bitch if you ever think about getting the authorities to come invade my shit like how your momma did Ms. Juanita; just know that I'm going to tear your white ass up and show you that I'm not the bitch to be fucked over." While Katherine Watson stood with her face twisted up with nothing to say. Fallon then gathered the girls and backed away while saying "let that be a warning and by the way good luck on finding that bill trick." As Fallon and the girls walked out while delivering a couple of snaps of the fingers when exiting the office. Katherine Watson then rushed towards the door and shouted out "Grace your fired" and slammed the door. While she stood leaning up against the door to catch her breath she then ran over to her telephone and made a phone call to the detectives unit and replied "I'm in need of an investigation on the Berkely Estates, these whores done struck again."

~Momma Joyce house~

While Fallon and the babes revenge plot on the conservative women's committee leader has come to an end for the night. Fallon then headed over to her mother's house to give her a hand with cleaning. Once Fallon entered the home and walked down the hall to her mother's knitting den, out came Rachel blocking the doorway. "Hey how's momma I picked up some more cleaning supplies" said Fallon, Rachel chuckles underneath her breath "do you think momma really wants to see you right about now," said Rachel. With confused look upon her face Fallon responds "and why is that, what's going on with momma", as Rachel blocked her from looking inside the knitting room she then replied "nothing, she's minding her business and knitting her a quilt" said Rachel. As Fallon gave up trying to look beyond Rachel she then said in a low tone "oh I see, so is this how it's going to be Ray? is this really how it's going to be." Rachel shrugs her shoulder's and replies "hey it is what it is."

As Rachel continued to block the doorway, Fallon then found strength to push her out the way so she can enter the knitting room. While Rachel went backing into the wall she then begun to shout "you have every nerve putting your hands on me; just like you have every nerve showing your face around here after two weeks momma been trying to get in touch with you." Fallon shouts back "I been here faithfully just because I got a little busy with life doesn't mean I neglected her; since you want to talk about missing in action where you been at?" "Work and spending time with my husband something you don't have" shouted Rachel, Fallon sticks her hand out in front of Rachel and replied "oh girl please I don't know why you think someone is worried about being married and how funny you show up when momma comes calling on me." As Rachel became upset, she then slapped Fallon's hand from in front of her and shouted "you better get your hand out my face", Fallon shouts "or what bitch, what in the fuck can you possibly do?"

As both of the sisters went back and forth with one another Momma Joyce then showed that she was through with them both as she screamed "stop it that's enough, I get so sick of this bullshit yall are sisters; but all you do is fight like bitches with an unbalanced hormone I'm tired and I want to be left alone." While momma Joyce rose from her chair and walked towards the hall to head to her bedroom. Fallon then touched her on her shoulder and said "momma I'm sorry", Momma Joyce replies "not today Fallon just go home." While Fallon and Rachel stood watching her go to her room, Rachel then said "you heard what she said go home." While Fallon frowned her face towards Rachel she then asked "you know you always couldn't stand me and I never understood why; why is that Ray, what is your problem with me?" Rachel responds the same problem

I always had against you "your never no help." As Rachel said what she needed to say and walked past Fallon with a bump to the shoulder. Fallon then turned looking down the hall at her and said out loud "I'm sorry that he hurt you and she didn't believe you but what was I supposed to do?" As Rachel grabbed her purse and stared down the hall at Fallon in the knitting den, with tears rolling down her face. She then rolled her eyes and walked out slamming the door behind her, leaving Fallon standing under a dim light unforgiven.

~The Pink Pony~

While boss lady Fallon stood hearing the screams and the tears that were, shed while reminiscing the night that Rachels life has changed forever. Down at the pink pony was no other than Kardea trying to fix where she has went wrong. While Kardea made her way into the club she happened to stand in the entrance way and took a look around the building. Once she finished gazing around the building, she then took a deep breath and walked over slowly to the bar. As she was slowly on her way over to take a seat with the rest of the girls. The girls that were posted up at the bar decided that they would distance themselves away from her by finding them somewhere else to sit. Once Kardea seen how the girls that she once known as her coworkers didn't want nothing to do with her. She quickly raised an eyebrow at them and taking her seat at the bar. As she sat down, she asked "now isn't that a bitch; like what's gotten into them thots", as Troy the bartender served her up her special of tequila and sliced kiwi's. He then replied "them hoes mad at you", as Kardea turned and looked at the females and turned back to Troy she then replied "I don't know what for, it wasn't like I was benefitting their ass anyway; literally between me and Sapphire we was the only chicks up in here that were getting to the bag."

Troy agrees with her as he said "yea', you are right about that you and Sapphire sure knew how to make them niggas spend all their cash." Kardea replies, "that we did, and we always found a way to put on a great show." As Kardea sat thinking about her time at the pink pony, Troy then asked her "so are you thinking about coming back?" Kardea sips her tequila and replies "to be honest it would be nice, but I don't think Tootie is going to let me get back on stage." Troy replies "well if that is your concern there is the woman you need to see." As the pink pony's owner Tootie came and sat next to Kardea she then said "you know I never thought to see your face back in here so soon." Kardea keeps a straight face as she replies "well here I am", as Tootie looked over at her she then replied "you know one thing I admire about you is your strength, your courage and motivation to keep going; you really is that girl Kardea and I do miss you but I can't allow you back up on that stage." Kardea becomes emotional as she becomes upset "and why not? I was your strongest dancer, your headliner of the night, I'm the one that held this club down right along with you."

As Tootie sat and agreed with every word that Kardea was saying she then replied "and that you were, and you did; but times has changed quick and in a hurry, while you were gone I took it upon myself to hire some new girls." Kardea replies in shock "new girls?" as Kardea sat in disbelief, Tootie then called over one of her new headliners. As the new girl came over and stood next to Tootie, Tootie then decided to introduce her to Kardea. "Violet I would love for you to meet someone, this is Kardea she use, to be one of my headliners here at the pink pony." As violet waved and said how she heard so much about her and tried to shake her hand. Kardea then slapped Violets hand out of her way and tossed her glass of tequila on to Tootie and replied "fuck this shit, bitch now you really don't have to worry about me." As Kardea snatched her purse and stormed out of the door, Tootie then replied underneath her breath "that ungrateful bitch." Once Kardea walked out of the pink pony with no intentions on apologizing, that night has become the last night that she would ever be able to return back.

Chapter 7. Sassy

As noon done set in on the next day and Kardea was on her way up the front porch to visit Fallon. She then wondered to herself about what was going on, as she saw men in colored safety vest's coming in and out of the home. While she made it inside of the home and seen Miracle coming down the opposite side of the hall. She then said to her "hey Miracle what's going on?", as Miracle shrugged her shoulders and mentioned how when she woke up that the workers were already at the home. Kardea then rushed quickly up the steps to Fallon's master suite and barged through the door in a panic "boss lady what's going on, who's all these men?" said Kardea. As Fallon sat up from laying back across the sofa she then replied "damn girl you barged up in here like someone was robbing the place; like someone has gotten you spooked." While Fallon rose from the sofa and turned off the television Kardea then replied "did something happen' like a fire or a leak; don't tell me these hoes are flushing their tampons" Fallon laughs as she heads over to her and said "girl no, there is no fire, no leak and damn sure no bitches flushing their coochie sticks." While Fallon stood face to face with Kardea she then replied "I made some alterations to Ladies Nights and let's just say that it's for the better."

Kardea replies "alterations, alterations like what?" as Fallon smiled at Kardea and stuck out her hand for her to grab ahold of it she then replied "I can show you better than I could tell you take my hand and come with me." As Kardea grabbed ahold of Fallon's hand and walked down to the lower level of the home. Fallon then stops her and replied "before I even take you down here just know that this is where a niggas true fantasies comes to life." While Fallon headed down the steps of the basement and told Kardea to follow her, Kardea then looked down the steps and slowly headed down behind her. As she made it down the steps and took one step on to the cold basement concrete, she then became amazed, as the basement was now transformed into a pole dance lounge. Kardea becomes overwhelmed as she looked beyond the strobe lights "oh my gosh I can't believe it, this cannot be happening right now." Fallon replies "oh, it's happening", in excitement Kardea replies "like how did you even get all of this?", Fallon responds "well let's just say that the extra money we made from grand opening was able to help us out with getting some new stuff."

As Kardea walked over and placed her hand on to the pole and looked up at how far the pole went to the ceiling. She then begun to imagine herself busting out every trick she could imagine while pleasing the fellas with her voluptuous body and her sexy ego. As she came from out of her trance she then turned towards Fallon while laying up against the pole and replied "so what made you add the poles" Fallon walked up to the stage and held on to the pole with her and replied "well, sometimes in life we have to be considerate to what a person brings forth to the table; and a person with potential and a passion deserves to have that." Kardea sighs while she replied "so you mean to tell me you did this for me?" Kardea turns and looks at Fallon and replied "yea I did, but also I did it to save Ladies Nights; since that bitch that runs the women's committee wants to shut us down." Kardea replies in shock "are you kidding me?", "I wish I was, but no; things are going to get real around here very soon, but I don't need you worrying about that only thing I need you to worry about is doing what you do best master that pole."

While Kardea looked up at the pole and told Fallon thank you, in came Miracle checking out the lounge. "Damnnn they did a good ass job; this is dope" said Miracle, Fallon smirks at Miracle and replied "well thank you, you know here at Ladies Nights we are all about doing big things." Miracle chuckles as she replies, "I see this is crazy; I love these red leather chairs." As Miracle rushed over to the lounge sofa and crashed down on them, she then said "this is the life", "well I'm glad you like it; it did cost a pretty coin" said Fallon. While Kardea swung around the pole she then said to Miracle "I wouldn't get to comfortable loving on that sofa if I was you; your job will be upstairs servicing the men fetishes like all the rest of the women." As Miracle sat up of the sofa and looked up at Kardea she then replied "that's cool with me, I see no problem with that." While Miracle sat back rubbing on the leather sofa and Kardea continued to swing from the pole. Fallon then steps in saying "actually Miracle will be working the pole", as Miracle sat up and placed a shocking look on her face. Kardea then came crashing down from the pole shouting "what, how is she going to work the pole and she don't even have any skills; this hoe doesn't even know how to cat crawl a pole she's not even a dancer." "Well by today and the end of this week she would be because I'm putting you up to training her," said Fallon. Kardea screams "what!!, "I'm sorry I don't mean to interrupt but I think I'm ok with working upstairs," said Miracle. As Kardea stepped to Fallon she then said "see you heard what she said she doesn't want to", "no Miracle is going to do what hell I tell her to do; this is not about what she wants to do and this shit is not up for debate so you train her" shouted Fallon.

Once Fallon walked away from Kardea and Miracle to head back up to the upper level of the home. Miracle then dropped on to the sofa and sighed with her arms folded, as Kardea took one more spend around the pole and replied "I feel you." She then came walking from off stage and dropped down on the sofa next to her. As Miracle felt uneased about her sitting next to her, she then decided that she would move over just a little to place a gap in between them. While Kardea caught on to what she has done she then chuckled and replied "bitch you can't be that serious, it's not like I'm about to jump up and bite your' ass." Miracle responds "well you just never know when it comes to you, you been attacking me ever since I got here and I still don't know for what reason." Kardea quickly replies, "there's nothing to know because there was never a reason", while Kardea sat with her elbows in her lap with her hands folded she then replied "I'm glad we are alone together because I would like to apologize for attacking you the way I did it was uncalled for and I should of never done that; I was a bitch and I guess I'm saying I'm sorry." While Miracle sat trying to figure out if she should accept her apology or not, she then replied "you know I never thought I would hear them words come out your mouth, you might be one sassy bitch but I can tell that you have a heart down in there somewhere." Kardea turns to Miracle and chuckles "damn who you supposed to be my counselor", Miracle replies "never that but one thing I can be is your partner, so are you going to teach this girl that can't dance how to master the pole or no?" As Miracle got up from the chair and showed that she was ready, Kardea then looked up at her and said "foe sho let's do it."

~Detectives Unit~

As Miracle was in position to learn how to master the pole with the help of the leading lady, down at the detectives unit was no other than Katherine Watson trying to sabotage the women of Ladies Nights. As she stood with little information needed in her hands like a brochure of the Berkley Estates and the sellers contract between Brad and Fallon. She then urged the chief to investigate Fallon, as the chief taking a look at the sellers contract and wanted to know how she was able to get it. She then replied "my husband he is a realtor", as the chief looked at the signed contract he then asked "may I ask you; did your husband hand you over this contract." Katherine replied "no I kind of just popped in his office and took it", while the chief shook his head and handed back over the contract he then replied "I'm sorry Mrs. Watson but there is nothing I can do for you; if your husband didn't give you consent then I can't start an investigation."

While Katherine stood patting her foot out of frustration she then replied "now Rick I done known you for several years and I know that you are capable of handling a lot of cases behind the scenes and under the table; It wouldn't be a pretty sight if I would have to break my promise to not say anything to the higher ups." As Rick sat looking at her, he then placed his head down and said in a low tone "Katherine what is this about why does this house that your husband made a pretty good profit on affects you so much? the house been abandoned for years." Katherine leans in and says in low tone "it's because he sold to a crook, supposedly this woman that goes by the name Fallon tricked him into letting her buy the home; just to turn it back into what our city doesn't want which is a whore house." As Rick took the papers from Katherine and mentioned if it was really a whore house. Katherine then went deep into her purse and slammed down the article about the grand opening of Ladies Nights. Katherine raises her voice "look it's right there; it's written right there how can you not be disgusted by this?"

While Rick went through the news article reading the headlines and viewing the photos. Katherine then pulls out her phone and Said's in a harsh tone "and that's not all look at this mess; can you believe it, there's videos of women degrading themselves and gold mouth thugs just waiting to be blown, Uggh." As Rick leaned back in his chair and looked at Katherine become frustrated by the naked women in the video. She then shouts "please don't look at me like that I'm not in the wrong here", as Rick asked for the bill she spoke of earlier about the brothel home being veto out by the women's committee and the court. She then replied "the bill happens to be nowhere to be found; but I'm sure with your title you will be able to be granted a copy from the courts." Rick replies "I don't know Kathy this may be a little tough to do", as Katherine leaned in close to his ear she then said in a low whisper "I'll pay you 40k and have your money by the end of the investigation but that's only if you agree to get the job done."

As Rick thought about it to himself, he then grabbed ahold of the newspaper and sellers contract and handed it off to one of the officers that works beside him. As Rick allowed Mrs. Watson to have power over him by agreeing to the investigation so he would not be exposed for whatever she knows about him. He then tells her that he would get right on the job and have some information for her as soon as possible. Once Katherine stood soaking it all in, she then turned her back towards him and headed out of the office without saying thank you. While Rick mumbled under his breath "what a bitch" he then spined his chair around and told officer Nathan to find out what he can about Ladies Nights and Fallon. As Nathan went through the article and went through the sellers contract reviewing the information that was listed in order to approve for the home. He then came across a Photo Id of Fallon and closed the contract, as he was in disbelief that the woman, he was falling for might be a fraud.

Chapter 8. The Trap

While the babes of Ladies nights were gearing up for another spectacular night in the brothel. The other women noticed that miracles do come true as Kardea, and Miracle placed their differences to the side. To master the pole together for a night that Fallon was planning for in a couple of weeks. While Miracle dropped down from the pole into a split and wiggled her cheeks. Kardea cheered happily as she shouted out "yasss bitch you better work; girl you are ready", as Miracle stood up from the floor of the stage. Everybody then cheered her on while they applauded her and said how great of a job she has done. While Fallon stood watching on, she then shouted out "I see yall; yall is ready, great job you guys." While Miracle and Kardea walked from off the stage and made their way over to Fallon, Fallon then stood with a smile upon her face and replied "you guys killed it, that was just completely amazing."

As Miracle thanked Fallon and Kardea, Fallon then replied "no thank you because I just found what I needed." As Kardea responded "and what was that?" Fallon than called over Sapphire to join them and replied "stripper bowl Sunday is in a couple of weeks and you three are going to be my headliners for that night." While Sapphire jumped up and down in excitement, Kardea then replied "oh shit; we in this bitch foe real. As Miracle stood looking at them enjoy the good news, Miracle then replied "if you don't mind me asking what is stripper bowl Sunday?"

Sapphire shouted "gurl you never heard of stripper bowl Sunday?", Miracle shook her head no and stood waiting on an answer. "Stripper bowl Sunday is one of the biggest nights; one of the nights that the ballers come out and stacks are thrown while these niggas are drunk off their asses" said Kardea.

Miracle replies "so what your saying is that men would come and just spend a couple of dollars just to see us dance." Fallon steps in and replies "no what she is saying is that men would come and spend their last dime to see you perform there's a difference". As Miracle stood thinking about what she said, Kardea then replied "you'll get it little mama just make sure to rack and protect your stack." As Miracle thanked Kardea for the encouragement and headed over to talk with the other babes. Kardea and Sapphire then headed back upstairs to room 6 and begun to undress out of their dance attires. While they were in the room pulling out their outfits for later that night, Sapphire then received a text message from a dude name Reiko. As she read the message to herself, she then turned to Kardea and leaned back up against the wall and sighed.

As Kardea turned back and looked at her, she then lifted her eyebrow and said "girl you sure is over there quiet who done got you in a mood." Sapphire looks at Kardea and replied, "it's Reiko, he wants to see us", Kardea replies, "well tell Reiko that we aren't coming we have better shit to do." Sapphire sighs as she received another message from him offering 10k to please him and his boys. "He just offered 10k" said Sapphire, Kardea replies "I see that Reiko still hasn't changed a bit, oh cheap ass." As Kardea chuckled at Reiko's offer Sapphire then said how she could use the money to help out with her boyfriend's shop. Kardea laughs as she replied "I guess anything for that barbershop huh, what bitch you know goes hard for a nigga they just met at the club." Sapphire leans up from against the wall and responded "if you don't want to do it just say that", Kardea replies, "it's not about if I don't want to it's about how to settle." As Kardea grabbed a towel and wrapped it around herself to go freshen up she then said "were going to Reiko's but they better be up for a different occasion; now excuse me as I go wash this kitten." While Kardea left the room to go wash up for the night, Sapphire then checked her phone and responded to the message with "will be there."

~8 mile~

As the ladies made it to the home of Reiko and the Dayton Street hustlers, Kardea and Sapphire made their way towards the home in the all black silk half tank top an leggings. As Kardea stood side by side with Sapphire, she then looked over at her and said "you ready?", Sapphire responds "yeah, I was born ready." As Kardea rang the doorbell and pounded on the door, she then turned towards her and replied "that's my girl." As Reiko came and opened the door to let them in, he then replied "damn girl I almost thought I was going to have to hide the stash, yall sounding like them boys." Kardea replies "what's up daddy" as Reiko looked down at Kardea and lured his eyes all over her body, he then allowed them to come in. While he watched them from behind saying "damn yall looking thicker every time I see you", as Sapphire laughed at Reiko she then replied "boy you are crazy where shall we sit. As Reiko told the boys to give up their seats for the ladies, Sapphire and Kardea then made their way over to the sofa and took their place.

While Kardea and Sapphire sat to themselves on the sofa while watching the other men play dominos and cards. Reiko then grabbed a bottle of Hennessey and crashed down in the middle of them. As he placed both of his arms around the ladies, he then decided to offer them both a drink "how about a drink; I feel as you can use one or two to loosen up. While Kardea told him to pour her up a cup, Sapphire then refused as it was her turn to be asked. As she refused the cup of Hennessey, Kardea then turned to her and gave her a look. As Sapphire seen the look that Kardea was giving her she then looked at Reiko and replied "on second thought I would actually love to, I don't even know why I said no." Reiko cheers her on "hell yea that's what the fuck I'm talking about" as he gave her, her cup, both Sapphire and Kardea looked at each other and quickly smiled. As Reiko downed his drink, he then went back to placing his arms behind their backs and begun to rub them on their sides saying "so did you guys coming over here to talk or did you come over to be fucked by the gang." As Sapphire quickly downs her drink she then replied while leaning in feeling on him "we came for the whole experience", "and we mean the whole experience" said Kardea.

Reiko looked at both of them and replied "well if yall two came for the whole experience, then it seems as a nigga got some pipe laying to do", as the girls chuckled and leaned up from his chest. He then offered them to hit a blunt, as the ladies looked at one another and shrugged their shoulders they then replied "sure." While Reiko begun to grind up the weed and rolls his first two blunts', from the table shouted one of his homeboys "man fuck that tired ass blunt we hungry for some pussy nigga." Reiko replies "man shut your punk ass up "as Reiko stood up from the couch and turned towards the ladies, he then told them that they would finish up the blunts in the room. While Kardea and Sapphire were ok with his choice, they then rose from the couch and followed behind him. As the other men that were sitting playing dominos and cards became frustrated and started talking sideways. Reiko then came backout the room and said "you niggas bets to calm that shit down, yall going to get some pussy just hold up and let a real nigga smash first." While the other men fanned Reiko off and whispered underneath their breaths, Reiko then placed his blunt back into his mouth and laid back on to the bed and replied "I swear if you haven't hit no weed like this before; then you bitches don't know what you are missing, this shit would have you lit in less than 8 minutes".

As Kardea stood up from the bed she then begun to strip out of her top exposing her boobs to grab his attention. Once she begun to play with them Reiko then happened to watch on while he begun to strip out his shirt. Once Kardea was up and gripping her boobs to turn him on, Sapphire then decided that she would join by stripping down out of her top as well. While both of the ladies were moving side to side as they moaned and gripped their boobs, they then told him to strip. As the directions was giving to him, he did just that by pulling down his pants and waiting on the next command. As he stood watching them while smoking the last of the blunt, Kardea then walks up to him and smacks the blunt out his mouth and replied "fuck boy didn't I tell you take that shit off", as Reiko smiled at her Sapphire then replied "she don't see nothing funny , take that shit off." While Reiko submitted to the order of Kardea and Sapphire he then removed his draws and laid back on to the bed. As he laid there faded and excited about him getting some pussy he then replied "I got what you hoes need come work my dick." As Sapphire walked over to him and stood between his legs she then said "yes sir but before we work the dick, can you tell us how you would like it worked."

While Reiko laid back enjoying the satisfaction of two woman seducing him, he then replied "one of you could sit on my face, while the other swallow up my balls." While Sapphire looked back at Kardea, she then hesitated on what to say next, once Sapphire begun to choke. Kardea then stepped up to him and replied "whatever you ask for is what we shall do", once Kardea pushed him back. He then grabbed ahold of her and begun kissing her on her neck, while Kardea was getting a load full of kisses upon her neck, Sapphire then squats down and begins to feel on his balls. Once he begun to moan to himself and seemed to be enjoying the wetness from her pussy placed in her hands and wrapped around his balls. Sapphire then passes a gun to Kardea and grabs one of his bandanas from off the shelf. As Reiko stopped kissing on Kardea neck he then placed his two fingers on the inside of her pussy and begun to finger her. As Kardea looked back at Sapphire she then winked at her and moaned "ah it's so good ahh fuck Reiko", As Reiko begun to put some rhythm into his finger tips and begun to finger her with a little more speed. He then looked passed Kardea and said to Sapphire "damn bitch where you at I told you to suck a niggas balls the fuck", as Sapphire stood in the corner smiling she then pulled out a gun and pointed it at him. As Reiko noticed the gun, he then tried to push Kardea off of him; but noticed that he was held at gun point by her as well as he was fingering her out.

As Kardea held the gun to the side of his head and gave him a few kisses she then replied in a sexy low tone "nigga if you ever thought 10k was going to get us fucked by the gang you have us fucked up, now stand the fuck up." As Reiko stood to his two feet he then tried to holler for help, before he was able to do so Kardea then told him to get on his knees as Sapphire stuffs his mouth with a bandana. Once Reiko was on his knees slobbering over the bandana as he tried to talk, Kardea then replied "I'm going to give you a chance to talk but if you don't tell us where the money is at I will be force to pull the trigger, Now speak motherfucker." As Kardea held the gun to the side of his head and pulled the bandana out of his mouth. He then replied "look I'm telling you hoes this isn't what you want", Kardea shouts "nigga if I get to capping in this bitch it's going to be what you don't want, now where's the money?" Reiko yells "I don't know", as Sapphire walked up to him and punched him in his face, she then said "look bitch you got me fucked up; tell my sis where the money is at or I would be force to take out one of your boys." Reiko looks up at her and replies "look bitch you aren't about to do shit", as Sapphire looked at Kardea and then back at him she then walked over to the bedroom door and opened it. "you better not you bitch" said Reiko, while Sapphire looked out into the living room and checked out the boys she then called over one of his boys name Big Boi.

As Big Boi saw that Sapphire was luring him to the room, he instantly took himself out of the game of dominoes and hurried over to her. While he headed over to her, he then replied "today is your lucky day because I'm about to run in that pussy like a train", as Sapphire laughed at his remarks she then took him by the hand and brought him into the room while closing the door behind her. As he seen Reiko on his needs looking terrified, he then wondered what was going on "my dog what the fuck is this, yall role playing or something." While Big Boi stood confused about what was happening Sapphire quickly placed the gun up behind his head and told him to get on his knees. As Big Boi dropped down to his knees and Sapphire placed the gun to his head, she then looked over at Reiko and said "it's your chance to speak or ill blow his fucking brains out where's the money."

Reiko replies to Sapphire once more "I'm not saying shit", "man please tell this bitch where the money is I don't want to die man," said Big Boi. "If you do as he say, then we won't have to bust a cap in his ass" shouted Kardea, Reiko replied "do it shoot his punk ass." As Kardea looked over at Big Boi she then replied "I'm sorry" and pulled the trigger delivering a shot to Reiko's head but misses. As Big Boi screamed and started to shake due to him being nervous, he then begged them not to shoot him and told them that the money was under the mattress. As Kardea flipped over the mattress and found the 10k in a black trash bag. She then grabbed ahold of it and told Reiko and Big Boi to stand up, as they stood up from the bedroom floor. Kardea then told them to walk back into the other room an act like they enjoyed themselves. While Reko and Big Boi did just that, Kardea and Sapphire made a run for it out of the bedroom window and into the car to flee from the home.

 Once Kardea and Sapphire was able to make a run for it, back at the trap house Reiko became highly upset with Big Boi and delivered shots to his chest 5 times, telling him to go to sleep after he told Kardea and Sapphire where the 10k was at. While the girls were able to escape Kardea dropped off Sapphire back at home to lay low while she laid low at the brothel. Once Kardea gave Sapphire her portion of the money Sapphire then replied, "bitch I would of never thought we would be able to pull this shit off; but we did we got paid today bitch." As Sapphire thanked Kardea and exited out of the car, she then ran up to the house and headed inside to tell her boyfriend about the good news. Once she made it to the bedroom and found him laying down watching TV, she then poured the money out on to the bed and shouted out loud "we rich bitch."

As night has fallen and Ladies nights was off to a successful night, Fallon then took her seat behind her desk to take a breather and to watch the money come in. While she was sitting to herself quietly a man came up to her and asked if she knew what room wasn't getting any action. As she got up from her chair and pulled him by his ear, she then walked him over to room 7 and replied "now all momma needs for you to do is to enjoy the experience. "As Fallon opened the door for him and allowed him to walk in while closing the door behind him. He then replied, "damn girl you bad as fuck; you must be new", As Miracle walked over to him, she then replied, "I need you to shut up and tell me what you're here for." As the man handed over the cash and Miracle counted it, she then smirked at him and picked up her paddle while telling him to strip. As the man stripped out of his clothes quickly, he then kneeled on to the heart shaped bed and told her that he's been a bad boy.

While Miracle looked at the paddle and at his perfect plumped ass, she then laughed and said to herself "this shit been getting freakier by the minute." As Miracle swung the paddle and delivered 5 spanks to his ass cheeks he then got up from the bed and paid her a flat rate of $250. Once Miracle looked at the cash that was placed in the palms of her hands, she then replied, "what's this for." As the man pointed up at the sign on the wall, she then became nervous as the sign read pussy eating. While she looked back at the 250 and looked at him, she then took a deep breath and laid on to her back. As he spreads her thighs apart and begins to kiss her between the inner part of her thighs, she then begins to moan as she rubbed his head saying that his kisses were so warm. As he gripped her thighs tight and went to suck her pussy. Miracle then closed her eyes and begun to grip the sheets while she bitten her bottom lip to his tongue game being good.

While Miracle moaned like a wild woman as she was getting her pussy ate, dudes that were lined up for a ladies' nights experience begun to feel on their dicks as they heard how good Miracle was. As the men were excited and shouted, they wanted a taste of Miracle, Kardea then walked by and said to Fallon "guess the newbie done finally broke herself in." As Fallon laughed, she then replied, "I guess she has, now Kardea I don't want no shit between you and Miracle after she finishes up getting her pussy licked." Kardea responds "there's no reason to hate these niggas know where to come to find the best hood pussy in Detroit." As Kardea walked off down the hall, out came Miracle with a total of $450. As Fallon looked at the cash she then replied, "hold up how in the hell you make all that money off of a nigga eating pussy."

Miracle chuckles and replies, "he said he loved the way I taste and offered to keep going so I up the price on him and got me an extra $200" As Miracle placed the cash in Fallon's hands, she then headed outside to catch some fresh air. While Miracle headed down the porch and walked around the gate to have a cigarette. Out came Pablo from around back of the brothel snatching her around the neck and whispering to her to not make a sound "do not make a fucking sound or ill strike you said Pablo." As Miracle stayed quiet and did as he said Pablo then replied "did you think that I was stupid, did you think that I wasn't going to find you" as Miracle tried to speak Pablo squeezed harder around her neck and replied "so this is what you do?, you leave the man that clothes you that feed you and take good care of you to work in a whore house to be smutted out." As Pablo yelled and screamed in her face, she then said to him "what's the difference as she tried to gasp for air.

As Pablo held on to her by her neck and looked down at her he then smacked her across the face into a fence and said "don't you ever speak to me like that again". As Kardea and security came rushing down the steps of the home as they seen what has happened. Security then jumps on Pablo and begins to choke him up while telling him to leave the property. As the security guard tossed Pablo into the road Pablo then shouted "baby you see what he did to me; your just going to stand there and let this big motherfucker get away with it." As Miracle stood silent looking at him while tears fell from her eyes, Kardea then gave her a hug and walked her back inside. While Kardea held on to Miracle and took her into the kitchen she then looked in the freezer and pulled out a cold pack to go up against her face. As Kardea placed the cold pack on Miracles left cheek, Miracle then thanked her for helping her out "thank you," said Miracle.

As Kardea takes a deep breath and sighs she then replies "how long has this been going on", Miracle replies "two years now and I feel so a shame; I don't even know how he even found me." As Kardea held on to one of her hands she then replied "don't be, there is plenty of girls out there right now that are going through what you are going through; and some are going through worst situations where they are not even making it out alive, you happen to be one of the lucky ones." As Miracle asked about her face and if it was bruised from the slap, he gave her. Kardea then removes the ice packet and replied "I believe we have kept the spot from swelling you're going to be ok." As Miracle hopped down from the kitchen counter and stood with a dry towel dabbing her eyes from the tears that were shed. She then reached out and gave Kardea a hug and thanked her for everything.

~The Picnic~

While Kardea and Miracle were off to starting a new bond, there was one person that believed in being at odds and that person was no other than Mrs. Katherine Watson herself. As hundreds of people gathered in the park to celebrate the coming of an end to abortions. Katherine Watson made sure that her name was put out to the public to be known on her contribution to the city. As people continued to walk through the gates of the picnic Katherine then hopped in place in so much joy "this is impressive people are really showing up and the crowd continues to get larger by the minute," said Mrs. Watson. As Mrs. Watson stood looking into the crowd, while watching the people enjoy their plates of food and drinks. In came no other than Mrs. Watsons former receptionist Grace, as Katherine seen her walking up to her with a smile upon her face. She then pushed her assistant out of her way and replied "what a surprise to see you here." As Grace stood with her arms folded in front of her, she then replied "now why wouldn't I be here." Mrs. Watson replies in a sharp tone "because I fired you weeks ago", as Grace felt the rage and anger spurring from Katherines mouth she then replied "I'm sorry Mrs. Watson I didn't mean to make you upset I just thought that I was doing the right thing; and by showing up to your event I thought that it would make you happy."

As Mrs. Watson stood looking at Grace with nothing hardly to say she then smirked at her and said "thank you for coming, you really have a way of showing your gratitude towards others." Grace responds "well thank you, I believe that has been the nicest thing you have ever said to me", as Mrs. Watson made a straight face at Grace she then replied "oh darling do not flatter yourself; if you're going to be here please go and help yourself to some BBQ ribs or a cold cut sandwich with some potato salad." As Katherine easily pushed on Grace to leave from around her, she then looked at her assistant and replied "I can't believe I am allowing her to stay." While Katherine assistant watched her bicker about Grace, she then tapped her on the shoulder and said "Mrs. Watson it's your time to speak, go knock'em dead." As Katherine turned and looked up at the stage before the announcer called her name. She quickly rushed to the side of the stage and taken a deep breath, while she stood waiting to be called, she then turned to her assistant and asked about her attire. As her assistant gave her the thumbs up that she looked great, she then was called to the stage to greet herself to the crowd and to go over Pro-Life anti-abortion rights and laws.

As she made her way to the center of the stage and looked into the crowd she then waved and told everyone who she was, and how she created the women's conservative committee. As she made it aware that the committee stands for the American women and to protect them, she then shouted out to the crowd that as a city they should stand with them and to choose pro-life over abortions. As the crowd applauded her and she started to get into the topic a little deeper. In came Fallon and her girls dressed in pink t-shirts with the words Brothel Babes written across and a pair of daisy dukes. As they marched through the gates of the picnic and held up signs that said that Katherine Watson was a fraud and that she's a closeted democrat. Katherine Watson then replied from the stage "and look what we have here; if it isn't the over sexualized women from the Berkley Estates." As Fallon stared her down and continued to chant harder, Katherine then looked over at Grace and replied in anger "youuu" and walked off from the stage. Once Katherine made it down the stage, she then was greeted by the babes of Ladies nights and Grace. "Where you off to heffa" said Fallon, Katherine becomes shock to see them as they made their way past security.

    As Katherine stares all of them down she then replied "I know what you little whores are trying to do but I promise you your plan will not work" As Fallon stepped to her she then replied "you think you know but in all honesty you don't know our plan; but this right here is the start of it." As Katherine got up in Fallon's face she then replied "well, let the beginning begin so I can come right behind you and shut you down." Fallon responds "Katherine I know that you been having quite some issues lately, but don't let club ladies Nights be one, because one thing about us we will come to collect." While Katherine stood and smirked at Fallon she then replied "you're a strong woman; but just not strong enough to handle me, if I was you I'll be watching for what happens next and that goes for all of you." Fallon shouts "bring it bitch."

    As Fallon backed away from Katherine Watson and continued to have the girls chant pro-choice matters. Fallon then waved at Katherine and chuckled while replying "feel my wrath Mrs. Watson, feel it." As Grace stood on the sidelines watching, Katherine then walks over to her and starts shouting "it was you how dare you bring them to my picnic, how dare you." While Katherine screamed like a mad woman and the crowd of people with their families watched on. Security then rushed in and got between Katherine and Grace protecting both from physically harming one another. As Fallon and the babes looked on from the trail Fallon then chuckled to herself and replied, "you just got to love when an innocent white bitch wants her revenge." As Fallon and the girls got a good glimpse of Katherine trying to attack Grace, they then waved at the crowd of supporters and laughed amongst themselves as they headed back to the Brothel.

Chapter 9. Blue

While the picnic disaster was a success and Fallon was satisfied with the outcome of embarrassment that Katherine Watson has received. She then took it upon herself to celebrate the night with a bottle of chardonnay, while she gets ready for a night out in town. As Fallon fixed her make up in the bathroom mirror and viewed her dress to see if it was fitting the way she wanted it to fit. She then received a phone call from her lead lady Kardea, as she answered the phone to see what she wanted. Kardea then replied, "umm Boss lady I have a bone to pick with you", as Fallon unplaced the phone from her ear and looked at it in a funny way she then replied back to Kardea saying "girl what bone and what is you talking about." As Kardea started laughing and saying repeatedly "you did that shit", Fallon then replied "girl wait, I'm not understanding what 'so funny, why do I have a bone thrown over my shoulder? Kardea continued to laugh as she said, "I heard what you guys got into at the picnic, I just wish I was there so I could do my part as well."

As Fallon laughed, she then replied, "so I take it that the girls must be roaming around the house, yapping about the situation that happened between me and that cold snake Mrs. Watson." As Kardea chuckled she then responded, "now you know some of these ladies can't hold water, so yes I heard all about it up and through here." Fallon replied, "well good, let's just say that the trick had it coming, and I gave her all the business." Kardea chuckled and replied, "as you should since the bitch wants to try to come for what you built", Fallon quickly responds "exactly." While Kardea sat on the side of her bed holding the telephone she then said, "I sure wish I was able to see her face; I'm sure that her committee and her supporters are very embarrassed." Fallon chuckles and responds, "them, more like her, the bitch was really wheeling in people with ribs and potato salad just to have them vote against pro-choice abortion, hopefully the community isn't too stupid to swing the opposite direction." "You just never know" said Kardea, as Kardea listened to all the rambling in the background that Fallon was making she then replied, "umm you must be at home because your sure is making some noise."

Fallon grabs ahold of her purse as she replied, "that I am but not for too long; I got a big night tonight." While Kardea sat thinking about what she could be possibly doing at 7pm and wanted to know if she was coming into Ladies Nights for the night. Fallon then declined and said tonight it's not just a date it's a date with talent." Kardea replied "seems like someone found them some eye candy", Fallon chuckles and replied, "eye candy is the word but not for little owe me; if you must know tonight, I am going to be out searching for a new member, someone with flavor, that's vibrant and Hella colorful." Kardea replies slowly "wait, wait, wait just a minute are you thinking about adding men to the home." Fallon responds, "not just men, men that are willing to provide the experience just as good as you ladies do it." While Kardea sat back and laughed she then said, "well seems like the boss lady has her hands tied, hopefully he will be a smart choice and that will help bring women to ladies Nights; but if not there always room for me to slide in." Fallon replies, "hopefully isn't the word but we shall see, and girl what do you mean by slide in! because the only direction I'm going to see you slide in is to the left."

As Kardea laughed with Fallon an asked why, Fallon then replied, "because the men you're looking for don't work at Angie's." As Kardea came to a pause, Fallon then replied, "it's time to take another step up in this Brothel and by recruiting the gays, I would be able to incorporate a LGBT night and come out with a bag that I can't hardly lift over my shoulders." As Kardea was left speechless she then replied "what about us? And what about the men that come to see us, you sure that's not going to take away from us and cause a problem with the men that doesn't view that way." Fallon replies "girl bye nobody is stunting any man that has a negative thought to spill upon a gay man, if so then the nigga must be suspect himself; I just feel that it's time for a little flavor added to the house and if any man feels uncomfortable with that, they know what to do, like they don't do it anyway." While Kardea sat on the phone in shock she then replied, "it's time to hustle hard", While Fallon replied, "and momma is going to hustle even harder."

~ Club Angie's ~

As people started to crowd the bar and filled every table, that was set up around the dance floor. Fallon then made her way over to the bar in a hurry to take a seat. As she pulled out a stool and took her seat, she then looked around the bar in search of some sexy men. While she flipped her hair back and sat quietly to herself scoping out the area. She then became excited as she seen a nice brown skin man with muscles compatible to a body builder, heading to a pole in a yellow speedo. Once Fallon was about to leave her seat to approach him in came more men walking out of the dressing room, dripped down in nothing but Melanin and raunchy attire. As Fallon watched on from her seat a woman next to her shouted "oh baby I can't wait to see them take it off", as Fallon looked at her and cracked a smile, she just knew that having a couple of men would bring attention to the home. While she continued to watch the men head up to the stage to take their places, there was a bartender that came walking over and offered to take her drink order. As Fallon sat and ordered a ruby red, the bartender wasted no time on preparing it and made sure that he added an extra slice of kiwi and pineapple.

While the bartender sat the drink behind her and watched her be entertained by the fellas that were giving an early performance. He then got her attention by saying "Ms. Instead of doing all that jumping and hollering, you should be chasing this drink because you sure seem thirsty." While Fallon spins around in the bar stool she then looked at him up and down and replied, "come again", the bartender replies, "you might want to chase that drink." Fallon replies, "I heard you the first time" and smirked at him. While the bartender went on to serving 5 more people that sat around the bar, Fallon then cuts her eye at him and calls him over to her. As he went walking back over to her, he then leaned over the counter and replied, "so how I may help you again." As Fallon looked into his eyes she then replied, "with an apple martini and a conversation between me and you." As he laughed, he then replied, "I can definitely fix you up a martini; but on the second option I am off limits." As he turned his back towards her and begun to fix her a second drink, she then replied, "I wasn't talking about intimately, I was talking about business."

As he turned back around and slid her drink over to her, he then leaned over and replied and what type of business would you want to discuss with me about. Fallon replies," a business where your able to gain stacks of cash and never have to look back", as he stood in one place thinking about what she was talking about, he then said, "oh really and how much money are we talking?" Fallon chuckles and replies, "I'm talking about thousands of dollars just in one night to a week." "So, you're a businesswoman," said the bartender. Fallon takes a sip of her drink and places it down on to the table "I'm more than just a businesswoman I am the woman; and this woman here is out scouting for men to fill her club that she just rebranded." As the bartender fixed himself to a drink he then sat behind the bar in front of Fallon and replied, "so you a club owner what club?" Fallon replies, "it's not an actual club but Ladies Nights has the hype as one; let's just say is more of a naughty room." As the bartender took a sip of his drink he then replied, "so what type of dudes are you looking for; because you sure isn't going to find any hunk straight men in this bar." Fallon laughs and replies, "I see, but a girl like me can use a little diversity; you see my house is full of sexy woman that don't mind chasing a bag, and who says that a man can't stand beside her and hustle up a stack together."

While the bartender sat thinking about Ladies Nights, he then looked at Fallon with a shocking look upon his face "wait a minute, now that you done said a house full of girls, I know exactly who you are' don't you go by the name Fallon, but everyone calls you, boss lady." Fallon responds, "I am she, but if you don't mind me asking who is he?" "The name is Blue" said the bartender, Fallon responds "interesting, why Blue?" As Blue stood up from the stool behind the counter he then replied, "that was the nickname my mother gave me before she passed away; she called me blue because every time I didn't get my way, she would say I always got blue in the face." As Fallon chuckled, she then said, "that is the cutest thing ever, hopefully you still got that fire living inside of you", Blue responds "till this day I'm still blue in the face." As Blue looked at his watch, he then told Fallon how he needed to run for the night so he can get to his second job. As he picked up his duffle bag from behind the counter and placed it on to his shoulder. Fallon then stops him and offers him a ride, as he declined Fallon's offer, she then gave him a card and told him that if he ever wants to stop by and check out Ladies nights that he was welcome to. As Blue took the card and took one look at it, he then stuffed it into his pocket and thanked Fallon for her time.

~Sensations~

Once Blue left from Club Angie's and headed over to Sensations, there he was trimming his nails that have grew in and moisturizing the body before putting on a show. As he was preparing himself in the locker room, he then sat down at the vanity and pulled out a box of cigarettes to have a few puffs. As Blue did just that he then checked himself in the mirror and went to give a show. While Blue walked through the back halls of the building he then came to a door, which led to a room that was made into a square. As he entered inside of the room, he then took his place in the center of the square box surrounded by whips and a pair of black anal beads. While he stood quietly to himself behind the red curtain, in came a man on the opposite side of the curtains making himself comfortable. As the man sat down in the chair that was placed in the center on the room, he then pressed a green start button and waited for the curtains to open. Once the curtains opened there was blue squatting down and licking his lips.

As the man became excited, he then unzipped his pants and pulled out his penis and begun to stroke it. As he stared into the glass at Blue, while Blue was smacking his cheeks and teasing him every way he can. He then shouted for Blue to take his draws off and to throw them at the glass, as Blue did just that. The man begun to stroke his dick hard as he came up to the glass and placed one hand on the window as he was beating his meat. As Blue walked up to the window and begun to feel all over himself, he then picked up the whip and begun to whip the window as it stood for the guy that stood in a trance. While Blue crawled to the man and placed his hand over his hand at the window. The man that was in a trance begun to smile at him and decided that he would like to see more of him. As Blue looked over at the buttons that controls what viewers would like to see. The man then walked over and pressed the blue button for a live experience, as Blue seen the lights flashing for him to go service his client. Blue then rose up on to his two feet and walked out of the playroom while curtains in the back of him closed.

Once Blue headed out of the playroom, he then walked into a booth where there was a hole in the wall. As the man was signaled to head over to the gloryhole, he then walked over and stuck his dick into the hole and said in low scruffy voice "suck my dick good baby." While Blue seen the penis come through the hole and saw how hard it was, he then placed his hand over the white cock and begun to give it a rub down. Once he gave the dick a good rub down, he then placed the bulging hard cock into his mouth and continued sucking. While Blue was given a face full of hot sweaty cock, the client behind the wall was greatly satisfied as his head tilted back while he placed his two hands upon his hips. As Blue finished him off, he then took out his cellular phone while he was holding on to the man's cock and snapped a picture of himself. While the man's penis was still drizzling with cum in the palms of blue's hands, Blue then licked it up and said unto the man "thanks you can clean yourself up."

As the man headed over to the towel dispenser and grabbed a couple of napkins to wipe his dick off. He then met Blue at the door and admired his body saying "damn baby' I just love when you get dressed up for me", Blue replies, "oh really now; it's nice to know that my assets continue to get all of your attention." While Blues client begun to speak, he done walked up to him and placed his finger over his lips and whispered "Shhh" while sticking his finger in his mouth to have him taste the last bit of nut that he done got from out of his draws. Once the man licked and sucked on Blues finger, Blue then whispered in his ear "show me the money daddy." As the man went deep down in his pockets and pulled out the cash, he then placed It into Blues hands. While Blue counted it up and told him that he knows where the rest goes. As the man gave Blue, a kiss on the cheek and a smack on the ass, Blue then smiled and replied "be good daddy", "always" said the man.

~The Blue Romance~

As Blue finished satisfying a couple of men for the night, he then headed home to shower and to kick up his feet. While entering the home and tossing his duffle bag off to the side on to the ground. He walked into the kitchen and poured him up something to drink, as he took a sip of his water from the glass. In came Michael walking past him as he tried to say hello. While Michael went walking into the living area and took a seat on to the sofa, Blue then walked into the living area to check on him. As Blue went walking over to him and tried to hug on him, Michael then pushed him off and said "do you even deserve it." As Blue backed away from Michael unaware of what's going on between them, Michael then replied "so how long are we going to be doing this; because I'm sure the cushion beneath my ass is literally screaming." Blue sighs and replies "this must be about my job", Michael sighs and rolls his eyes while he stands up from the couch and walks away from him. As Blue turns around and grabs him by the arm he then replied, "I thought that you were ok with what I do! Michael turns to Blue and responded "there was a time that I was, but now it just seems like you don't have any time for me or for us; ever since you picked up this second gig you been home later than usual." Blue sighed as he looked into Michaels eyes "look I'm out here grinding; grinding for us", "all I have to say is that you were better off at the bar," said Michael.

Blue begins to raise his voice "shit you say the bar wasn't paying the bills; but this one is, baby all I want to do is help you and help us." As Michael kissed Blue upon his lips he then replied "you know what would help me right now", "and what's that" said Blue "you coming to bed and also saying that you would give up this side hustle down at sensations." As Blue thought about what to say to Michael, he then shook his head yes "ok if you want it, you got it but under one condition." Michael looks at Blue and replies "and what's that Mr.?" as Blue pulled out the card to Ladies Nights and showed it to him, he then replied, "if you say yes to me working here, I'll give up not just working at sensations but the bar too." As Michael took the card away from him and viewed it for himself, he then asked Blue what was it about." As Blue taking a deep breath he then said "Boss lady is looking forward to recruiting some males for her home and she invited me to come take a look to see if I would be interested." "When you say home are you referring to a Brothel?" asked Michael, Blue replied, "pretty much but look, I'll be able to be home in the morning and evenings until it's time for me to head back to work; also I wouldn't have to work two jobs just to make ends meet, Fallon said her ladies are doing numbers over there and I know all isn't coming from sucking no dick."

As Michael yawned while Blue was speaking, Blue then became upset as he felt that Michael wasn't paying him any attention. Blue replies "damn bae it's like that; see this the shit I was talking about last time." As Michael threw up his hands and rolled his eyes he then replied " baby stop I am listening to you I'm just tired; look if you want to work at the Brothel go for it, if you feel that it would benefit us then I see no problem with it." Blue responds back to Michael "look I'm trying my hardest here I know that ever since that day you were held at gun point, that you have been traumatized and living in fear for not just yourself but everybody; but as of right now I need you to fear no more because I need your support." As Michael looked into blue's eyes, he then gave him a hug and a kiss on the cheek and said "ok you got it now goodnight." As he headed into the bedroom and Blue stayed behind, Blue then took a look at the card in excitement while smirking and saying to himself "oh let's do it."

  As the next day arrived Blue was on to a new start as he awakened in bed stretching his arms to the air. Once he got done stretching, he then looked over at the clock and placed his two feet on to the floor and went to wash up for the day. Once Blue finished his shower and groomed up nicely, he then headed to the kitchen and grabbed a banana to go. As he was on his way out the door he then came to a pause as he thought about something humorous to leave for Michael. While he took a look at the banana and peeled the skin back, he then decided to take bite and leave the rest sitting on the table with a humorous letter written for his boyfriend Michael. Once Blue headed out and closed the door behind him, there was Michael standing in the hall rubbing his fingers through his brown sandy hair as he watched him leave. As Michael wondered what he has left behind he then made his way down the hall to the kitchen island and read the note that was posted on to the banana "finish me off." As he picked up the banana and read the note to himself, he then peeled the note off of the banana and said "well don't mind if I do sir" and bit into it. While Michael stood with the banana in his hand enjoying every bite and laughing about the humorous joke, he then walked back down to the bedroom and grabbed his vibrator while laying low under the sheets as he pleases himself to some, porn.

While Blue finally made it to the Brothel home there was Fallon standing in a beautiful lime green cat suit that even made Blue want to take a bite out of her. As Fallon welcomed him into the home and begun to show him around. Kardea and Miracle stood off to the side and mumbled under their breaths to each other as they watched on. "I take it that this bitch is serious" said Kardea, Miracle responds "oh she is definitely serious", as Fallon escorted him down to the lounge of the house, she then told him all about it. "This is where a man's dreams comes alive, I'm sure you know all about that since you been a bartender for all these years" said Fallon, Blue replies, "I know a little something and when it comes to dreams coming true, I know all about taking a man on a ride out his fantasy into his reality."

As Fallon chuckled she then said "well if you consider on becoming a babe you can make that possible", as Blue stepped on to the stage and swung around the pole he then replied "anything is possible and if I consider becoming a babe what do I get out of it." As Fallon sat back on to the couch and looked up at him work the pole she then said in a sexy low tone "you get to be that bitch; rack up these stacks and spend it however you fucking please as you are now considered my leading man." As Blue drops down from the stage and stands in front of her he then said "so since you would like me as your leading man how do we recruit these other dudes." As Fallon stood up from the chair, she then looks at him and replies, "by bringing them to you; consider this Thursday night to be all about you." As Blue and Fallon stood staring at one another Blue then replied "I'm no expert of a dancer but I do know how to rock a mic and collect bank, I accept now let's get to the money."

Chapter 10. Colored Blind

While Fallon was off to a good start by hiring the spit fire Blue to become her lead man of Ladies Nights. Katherine Watson was waking up on the brighter side of the bed, as she knew in her heart that justice would be served once Rick pulls a full investigation on Fallon and gathers all the dirt that she needs. As Katherine stepped foot outside of the bed and headed over to Brad she then sat on the edge of the bed and leaned over him and delivered kisses to his back. While Brad rolled over on to his back and saw her sitting on the side of him. He then looked up at her and said "good morning", as she sat with a smile on her face she then said "good morning" back and offered to make breakfast for them both. While Brad sat up and licked his lips, he then said to her "that sounds lovely my dear", as Katherine planted a kiss on his lips she then stood up from the bed and made her way towards the kitchen. While she entered the kitchen, she then shouted out to him "so what would you like for breakfast", Brad replies, "anything sounds good right about now; how about French toast with 3 slices of bacon I'll be up once it's finished, "said Brad.

As Brad placed his head back down on to the pillow and made his way back to sleep. In the kitchen was Katherine getting ready to make a lovely breakfast for two. As she warmed up the stove, panned up six slices of bacon and cracked open 3 brown eggs to dip the toast in. While she sliced up a couple of strawberries to top off the toast and poured some orange juice into a glass pitcher to put on chill. Suddenly the doorbell has rung with a couple of knocks, as Katherine took her time answering the door, she then made her way over to her flower pots that sat pretty in a corner that received a lot of natural light and decided to water them. As the door bell was pressed again and the sound of the bell echoed throughout the home. She then sat the water pitcher on to the counter and walked down to the door to see who it was. As Katherine wondered who could be standing at her front door, she then opened it to come to find out it was no other than Stephany.

As Katherine seen that it was her, she then questioned her about being at her home saying "excuse me but what are you doing here on my steps?", Stephany replied "I'm here to see Brad." In sarcasm Katherine replied "oh wow typical Stephany what's new you been seeing him off on for years now, don't you see that he has dodged the bullet", Stephany starts to become "frustrated me and Brad made arrangements now I'm here to see who I need to see I don't need you in my face smart mouthing me, we come in peace." Katherine steps to her and replied "oh you little young thing, you don't know a thing about coming in peace because all you been doing is causing trouble around here and far as smart mouthing goes I'm the queen of that I'm sure you knows that about now." While Stephany stood worried, looking past Katherine, Katherine then replied "looking for Brad he's busy matter of fact he's not even here, so I advise you to shoot I'm sure you get enough of fucking my husband." While Katherine steady harassing Stephany and telling her to leave her property, out came Brad taking a towel to the back of his head as his hair was still wet from his shower. Brad walks out the door in shock "Stephany", as Stephany looked over at Brad she softly spoken "hey", Katherine looks at Brad then at Stephany "what's going on here; is there something I'm not aware of?" As Brad looked at Stephany and Stephany cuts her eye at Katherine she then stepped to the side and grabbed a hold of little Isaiah's hand "somebody was in a big mood to see you today; hopefully papa is even in a bigger mood since today we made arrangements."

As Brad looked over at Isaiah and then at Stephany he then smiled and replied "hey son" as Isaiah looked up and seen that his dad was happy to see him, he then ran over to him and jumped in his arms while Brad gave him a kiss on the forehead. As Stephany stood smiling at Brad and Isaiah, Brad then replied "I'll get better at remembering next time", "you bet" said Stephany. While Katherine stood watching on with her hands, on her hips and tapping her left foot, she then frowned her face up at Brad and stormed into the house. While he watched her take off down the hall and made a left turn into the kitchen, Brad then looked at

Stephany and replied "don't mind her sometimes life has away with people", "I see" said Stephany. While Stephany stood playing with her nails with her head down, she then looks up at Brad and walks over to give their son a kiss and to say how much she loves him. Once she was finished, Brad then told Isaiah to run into the house to allow him and his mother to catch up with one another. As Brad turned towards Stephany, Stephany then said "he's growing up fast sometimes I can't believe that he's already walking; he looks just like you."

While Brad stood face to face with Stephany he then replied "I apologize for what I have done, I came to my senses and realized that maybe I was being selfish this whole time; I should of never came across the boulevard." Stephany smirks at him and responded "you couldn't help what you felt at that time; besides without you coming across the boulevard, I don't think I would have been blessed with my little miracle in there." As Brad thought about what she said he then started to feel a little much better, now that he knows that their son brings Stephany much joy and hope. As Stephany decided to say her goodbyes and walked down the walkway of the home. Brad then entered the home and headed down to the kitchen to see if breakfast was finished cooking "It smells so good in here." As Brad turned the corner entering the kitchen there was Katherine standing at the sink window watching Stephany leave from the home. While Brad stood quiet watching her, she then spoke out "so is this what life is coming to?" said Katherine. Brad rubs his fingers through his hair "look what do you want me to say or do", Katherine turns and looks at him and replies, "maybe nothing since the damage has been already done."

As Brad stood rubbing his face as he was trying to not show any expression of anger he then replied "I know what the problem is but how many times are we going to argue about the same thing", Katherine responds "I don't know maybe long enough until I say that I'm done", "can we just eat so I can take care of him" said Brad. As she folded up both of her arms and rolled her eyes she then replied, "eat' ha seems like the only one that's going to be eating around here is me since I missed out on several opportunities on being appreciated" As Katherine fixed her a plate of French toast and bacon she then sat at the head of the table and crossed her legs, while she dived in laughing and saying " your such a liar, you cheat and pretend to be so happy." While Brad stood watching her carry on with blaming him for their failed marriage, he then looks at her and said "you know what for a couple of years I have beaten myself up over a lot of things, but this time I'm not going to, especially not over you." As Katherine rolled her eyes at him, she then said "are you in love with her?", Brad responds "no and come on what type of question is that", Katherine responds "I couldn't really tell by the way you were looking at her and how you just allow her to show up to our house unannounced. Brad "raises his voice I have a kid with her", "exactly a kid with her instead of your wife."

 While Brad and Katherine were down each other's necks about Stephany and his infidelities, in came Isaiah tapping Katherine on the arm claiming that he was hungry. As Katherine looked over at him and smiled she then looked over at Brad and replied "how about I fix you some scrambled eggs, bacon and French toast I'm sure you would like that huh kiddos" as Katherine turned and looked back at him, she placed a big smile upon her face as she seen the most adorable smile that he has giving her. As Katherine told him to go play and stood up from the kitchen table to fix him a plate she then said to Brad "cute kid." Once Katherine fixed him a plate and placed it into the microwave to warm up. On came the breaking news discussing the abortion rights in America, as Katherine seen that they were getting ready to announce if the country stood with prolife and prochoice decisions. She quickly grabbed the plate of food out of the microwave and placed it down on to the table. Once she placed the food on to the table, she quickly ran into the living area and stood watching the television to hear the big news. Once she focused her ears in closely to hear what the supreme court decided on, she then said out loudly in excitement "I know that we did it, I know that the rules have been overturned." As the supreme court announced that pro Life anti-abortion laws were now in effect in a couple of states mainly in the south, Katherine then cheered and shouted out loudly "oh come on Michigan we can do this for our state."

As the news showed all of the states that were pro-life and pro-choice, she then saw that Michigan has not overturned their rules and views on abortions and decided to be pro-choice. As she stood feeling disgusted and in inferior as the news showed several advocates pushing for anti-abortion laws in the state of Michigan. She then turned off the television and replied "what a disgrace these people in the world are so wicked; and our own state did no justice by voting against the people that have stood for pro-life laws." As Brad sat at the table feeding Isaiah while listening to her ramble on about the people in Detroit, he then took a moment to shake his head and sarcastically say "maybe next time things would change, you'll definitely have my vote." As Katherine quit rambling and took one look at him, she then raised her voice at him as she replied "wipe that smirk off your face" while she became upset and stormed into the bedroom. As she stood in the bedroom with her back against the door taking a deep breath. She then happens to notice a gold paper sticking outside of a binder on a night stand in their bedroom on Brad's side of the bed. As she quietly tipped toed over to the nightstand and pulled the gold looking paper out of the binder she then stood in disbelief as she happens to realize that it was the bill that went against the Berkley Estates Brothel being ran in the city of Detroit. As she held the bill in her hand's she then smirked to herself and replied, "oh that bitch is going down."

~BlueNight~

As Katherine was on the verge of taking Fallon and her babes down, back at the Brothel stood blue in a dressing room fearing to hit the stage as the main act for pride night. As he stood adjusting his thong and gelling his hair in the mirror, in came the ladies Kardea, Miracle and Sapphire. As they entered the room, they all walked behind him and gave him a slap on the booty and told him to break a leg. As Blue looked at them in the mirror and begun to laugh Sapphire then replied, "you nervous?" "Now what type of question is that? Said Kardea, Blue turns around and leans up against the countertop and replies, "no lye I am kind of nervous; just to know that I am about to be in front of a crowd full of folks has me panicking." Kardea replies, well you can't panic for too long theirs too much money to be made; Sapphire go and get this man a drink." As Sapphire left out of the dressing room to grab Blue a drink from the bar, Miracle then excused herself as she went to tag along with Sapphire. While Kardea stayed behind to keep him some company she then took a seat and replied, "I remember my first night down at the pink pony, I was nervous than a motherfucker; the thing that tripped me out was how I became so comfortable once I hung upside down from the pole."

Blue responds "wait you use to dance at the pink pony?", Kardea replies, "dance isn't even the word, I performed." As Blue stood thinking about why she wasn't dancing at the pink pony anymore. He then decided to ask her "if you're not working at the pink pony anymore then why here?" Kardea looked up at Blue and said, "the pink pony was just to get by; but here this is where getting by turned into a sustainable hustle." As Sapphire and Miracle entered the room with some shots and a cup of crown royal for Blue. They then came into a circle as they wanted to make a toast to pride night and Blue headlining the event. As they raised their cups to the air and threw back their shots on the 3rd count, they then wished him good luck and went to find a spot. Before Kardea walked out of the dressing room she then turned back to Blue and replied, "I can tell that you're not a dancer, but little do you know you is a hell of a performer." As blue stood wondering how she would know that he has skills to work a pole. Kardea then walked over to him and replied, "it takes a real one to know one; remember when you hit that stage it's all in the thighs and legs that's what's going to hold you up." As Blue took Kardea advice and took another sip of his drink to ease his nerves. Kardea then said, "welcome to Ladies Nights" and headed towards the exit of the dressing room. As she was about to exit out Blue then stops her and replies, "I'm sorry that I have to correct you but it's a blue night and it's going down right here at Ladies Nights." As Kardea turned and looked at Blue she then cracked a smile and replied "and bitch you are absolutely right" while she made her way out of the dressing room to find a spot.

While everyone was making their way into the Brothel into the lounge, Fallon and the girls couldn't believe their eyes as many of people were showing up for pride night. As the lounge continued to have many of people coming through the door. Fallon then decided to tell security to stop accepting people due to the capacity. Once Fallon saw that the crowd was pumped up and ready for a show, she then ran over to the DJ and told him to get ready to spin something. As Fallon hit the stage and begun to welcome everyone to Ladies Nights. In the back stood Blue ready for his set until Michael came through the door to pay him a visit, as Blue guzzled down the last of his drink and seen Michael standing behind him in the mirror. Blue quickly turned around in shock saying "baby oh my gosh what are you doing here?" As Blue walked over and gave him a hug in excitement, Michael then replied "tonight is your big night and I am here to show my support; I see that the crowd is pretty hyped about you coming out, that's pretty cool." As Blue stood holding on to Michaels two hands, he then kissed his lips and told him to enjoy the show. Once Blue let go of his hands and begun to stretch before heading onto the stage, Michael then gave him a slap on the cheeks and told him to make sure that he got his ass clapping.

As Michael exited out of the dressing room and went to go take his spot down in the crowd, Fallon then announced Blue to the stage. Labeling him the sensational lead man of Ladies Nights and a sexy beta kitten for Pride night. Once Blue hit the stage in a sexy blue mesh thong and swung around the pole in a slow sexy pace. The crowd became stunned as everyone's mouths seem to have dropped when they saw how sexy Blue carried himself. While money was being thrown on to the stage and people were hollering and whistling for him to bounce some ass. Blue looked into the crowd at Kardea and did just that, as he used his thighs to climb the pole and begun to spin himself from the top of the pole back down to the base while nailing a split. He then looked at the money that was being tossed and decided to point out Kardea to have her share the stage with him. As Kardea tried to decline his offer, Fallon then looked at her and replied "girl this might be LGBT night and all about Blue but if the nigga is willing to share the stage with you to get that bread then why not!" As Kardea turned to Fallon and looked up at the stage she then snatched a shot off of the bartenders tray as she passed by and guzzled it down. Once Kardea seen how amazing Blue was at mastering the pole she then whispered to herself before hitting the stage "I told you your ass was a performer."

    While Kardea walked away from Fallon and hit the stage with Blue showing how they get crunked while mastering the pole together. The crowd went crazy as Kardea and Blue joined forces to deliver a special trick. As everyone was hyped up about the dual and money was being tossed on to the stage, from each and every direction of the lounge. Fallon stood proudly with a smile upon her face as she knew that she has ushered in a whole new wave of people. As Fallon stood watching Blue and Kardea tear the stage up, suddenly there was a tap to her shoulder. As Fallon turned around to see who it could be she then rolled her eyes and shouted "oh hell no, who in the hell done let you into my club; someone please get me security, security." As Katherine stood chuckling to herself, she then replied "oh darling that won't be necessary I was just paying you a friendly visit; I even bought me a drink, seltzer water would do a girl just fine." Fallon raises her voice "look heffa you been on to me real tough lately and it's starting to fuck with me; now why in the fuck are you here," said Fallon. As Katherine took a look around the lounge she then looked back at Fallon and replied "well, well , well now look who's upset; seems like the queen of the babes is pretty hurt butt, you showed up to my event unannounced so now I'm doing you a favor it's called karma."

As Fallon stepped to Katherine she then whispered "look lady I already told you this before you really don't want to rumble with me; so whatever you and your sick ass team is gathering together just know I'm ready and me and my girls will bite that ass." Katherine pretends to gasp for air as she pretends to be scared "oh wow I am so scared and what a threat, just know I take threats very seriously; but in all honesty you have a lovely lounge but I couldn't help but to notice the rooms that were made for pleasure on the top floor' it really screams Brothel." As Fallon snatched her drink from off the bartenders tray and took a sip she then replied "and what if I was to tell you that it was one, are you going to pay the cover charge and go get fucked out of your misery because if not what the fuck are you going to do about it" shouted Fallon. Katherine smirks at Fallon as she pulled out the bill "it's funny how your worried about me being fucked but it seems that in the end; the only one that would be fucked is you as your business takes a tumble," said Katherine. As Fallon looked down at Katherine's hands and seen the bill, Katherine then tells her to get a closer look at it. While she walked up to her and said softly in her ear "my husband may be a couple of things but one thing for sure that I know is that he's never been the sharpest tool in the box; I hope that you enjoyed being fucked by my husband." While Katherine backed away from Fallon's ear, Fallon angrily tossed her drink in her face and shouted for security to escort her out "somebody get this bitch out of my shit."

As security rushed over and tried to grab ahold of her Katherine then shouted "do not touch me; I may escort myself out." As Katherine rushed up to the top floor and stormed down the hall. She then shoved the door open to the brothel and pouted her way down the steps into her car." While Katherine walked away soaked in a blazer splashed with vodka. There was a man that walked past her into the Brothel looking to see if he could have a good time with a familiar face he can't stop thinking of. As security stopped him and asked for his Id, he then pulled out his wallet and flashed it to him quickly, as he turned around and was about to start walking towards the lounge. There was Fallon with her hand out "now you know that you are better than that hand over the ID or else", as he pulled out the ID card and placed it into her hands. She than took a close look at it and replied "you look more younger in your picture than you do in person but I'm not the one to judge, your cute Erick; now what type of experience you're in for tonight, we have hand jobs, blow jobs, a full fuck , a massage , feather tickling you name it and my girls got it." Erick responds "actually I'm not here for none of those", Fallon looks around the room then back at him and said "well what is it that you are here for because the party downstairs is over." As Erick scaled the room and saw Blue heading down the hall towards the entrance, he then looked at her and said "Blue."

    While Erick hurried over to Blue, Fallon then stood looking at the security guard with a grin on her face as she replied "that nigga said he here for Blue, let me find out that Blue got them white ding a lings chasing after him." As her and the security guard stood laughing about Blue tagging along the white meat. Erick then places himself up against the wall to move out of foot traffics way and to get to Blue easier. As Blue made his way down the hall with his boyfriend Michael holding him around his waist and talking about how great the night was, Erick then startled them both as he jumped out in front of them to get Blue's attention. As Blue held on to his chest as he was a little nervous about who was approaching them. He then looked shocked to see him as he replied in a low tone "Erick what a surprise what are you doing here?" as Erick looked into Blue's eyes he then said, "I'm here for you, how come you haven't come to see me?" As Blue looked at Michael then at Erick, Michael then butted his way into the conversation wondering who Erick was to him. Michael replies, "yo, bae who is this", Blue responds "baby calm down it's nothing serious and there is nothing going on he's just a regular from sensations that's all." As Erick sized Michael up and down he then raised his voice "you're questioning him about who I am who are you buddy?" Blue quickly gets in between them as everyone that was passing through started to stop and watch "look guys please don't do this right here this is so embarrassing," said Blue. Michael raises his voice as he becomes angry "embarrassing !? no what's embarrassing is this fucker stalking you at your job and by the way asshole I'm his partner what are you."

As Erick stood still and continued to look at Michael he then replied "partner he never told me about a partner", "well now you know so fuck off you douchebag" yelled Michael. As Blue yelled for them to stop he then turned towards Erick and replied "Erick I'm truly sorry but all you were was just a dance, someone that I sell a fantasy to; there has never been anything serious between us it was just strictly business." While Erick stood quietly looking down to the floor, Blue then replied "it's ok to pick up your head; I'm sure there would be plenty of men that would satisfy your needs." As Erick picked up his head he then responded "the reason my head was down is so I wouldn't have to look at you, you're a disgrace go to hell." As Erick turned his back towards Blue leaving Blue surprised about the reaction he has been given. He then made his way out of the home and went on about his business. Once Blue and Michael stood off to the side in the hall Michael then held on to Blue's Waist and said "thank you now are you're ready to head home superstar." As Blue replied "yes" and they headed down the hall to the outside of the home, walking up to them was nothing but trouble as Blue's brother stood at the gate with his two children watching them make their way down the steps.

Once Blue realized that his nephews were watching him exit out of a brothel home in nothing but a thong and a man on his arms. Blue then shouts as he was surprised to see them "Hakeem what are you doing here." Hakeem twisted up his face "the same I can say for you" said Hakeem, as Blue places his bag of bands down on to the steps and starts to put his robe on to cover up. Hakeem then laughs and said in a serious tone "nah you don't have to put that on we already seen everything want you go ahead and take it back off." As blue tied the robe in front and picked up his stacks he then replied "Hakeem what are you doing here and why do you have my nephews out so late."

Hakeem replies "don't worry about that worry about where you're going", as Blue walked down the steps and headed over to him, he then replied "what in the hell are you yip yapping about?" Hakeem snickers and replied "you just took the word out of my mouth; but the reason I am out here and my boys are out here with me is so I can show them what wickedness is upon my brother how you are sick." As Blue charged at him Michael then stepped in between them and told Blue to not do it. While blue stood back while Michael was holding him back, he then replied "you know Hakeem for a long time niggas use to tell me to be careful with you and that you have a lot of hidden agendas and people that you envy to, because you wish that you were able to walk in their shoes; just know if it wasn't for this white man standing in between us, just know that my size 9 foot would be so far up your ass that your children wouldn't even know what to do with you because you would be crying back to Jada like the bitch you are."

While Hakeem stood laughing looking at Michael and Blue he then said "wow strong words bro but your still a faggot, you not a real man; you just a pussy that refuses to watch his nephews to twerk his ass for a couple of dollars." Michael shouts "Hakeem stop it", Hakeem shouts "no what's he going to do", as Blue sighed and walked up to Hakeem and his nephews he then replied "just know that I love you guys and I work hard each and every day." As Hakeem took his two hands and pushed them back, Blue then kneeled back up and looked at Hakeem and replied " and to you love always wins no matter how big of a bigot you possibly claim yourself to be; and another thing this twerk money could do a whole lot more for your household then you ever could have done and you can ask Jada that one." While Hakeem stood silently as Michael and Blue walked off, he then gazed around at the people that stood upon the steps of the brothel and replied "What the fuck yall looking at", Fallon replies in laughter "a nigga who isn't a nigga but a bitch to his own bitch that takes care of him." "Homeboy your presence isn't welcome here now step" said security, "bye bitchhhhh shouted Kardea. As Hakeem snatched his kids by the hands and stormed down the street, Fallon then said in a low tone as she placed a cigar to her mouth "dudes claim they real men but argue like bitches."

Chapter 11. Positions

As Blue Night was a success down at Ladies Nights and money was to be made by both of the leading babes. Fallon then decided to treat herself to a new handbag and a carwash down at the express wash on 65th street. As she sat third in line for her Mustang to be handwashed and rinsed, she then sat back tight as she treated herself to a frozen popsicle that she bought from the minimart next door. While she opened the popsicle and placed it in her mouth and begun to lick and suck on the tip down to the base. She then happened to catch the wash attendants attention, as he stared her down while washing the roof of someone's car. As he looked over to his partner and told him to check out the view on Fallon working her lips around the creamsicle. He then through the towel at him and told him to wash up as he goes to shoot his shot. As Fallon seen that the wash attendant was on his way to her vehicle, she then rolled down her window and replied "don't tell me I'm not getting a wash today?" the car attendant replied "nah little mama you good, I just came over to introduce myself."

As Fallon smiled at the car attendant and rolled her eyes, he then replied "nah I'm serious my name is Brandon but everyone calls me Tripp." As Fallon chuckled and took a few licks of her creamsicle she then looked at him and said "it's nice to meet you Tripp I'm Fallon but everybody calls me boss lady." As Tripp stares into her eyes with a hard on in his pants from the way she was licking and sucking on her popsicle.

Tripp then looks down at his dick and begun to laugh while saying "boss lady and why do people call you boss lady?" Fallon looks him up and down and replies, "because I'm a bitch that gets shit done." As Tripp begun laughing and looking at her while nodding his head he then replied, "yeah I feel that shit that's what's up." While Tripp stood looking at her, he then said to her "well welcome to express wash our machines are down at the moment; but we going to take care of you with a handwash is that cool." Fallon looks over and smirks at Tripp as she replied, "yea that's cool." While Tripp was about to head back up the car line to car number two, Fallon then called his name and replied, "they call you Tripp? But what do you do to deserve that name you a rapper or something?" Tripp responds "nah I'm not into the rapping shit I slang and invest in businesses; if you got one maybe me and you could build a friendship and invest since you are technically a boss lady."

While Fallon laughed at Tripp's joke as she found it to be cute, she then replied, "that's not why I'm called boss lady, but I do own a playhouse on 52nd Berkley and Woodbine." Tripp rubs his hand across his face and replied "and what type of playhouse would this be", Fallon responds, "a brothel where we making every niggas fantasy come true." As Tripp stood feeling everything, she was saying he then replied "well damn it's like that huh", "foe sure" said Fallon. As Fallon and Tripp stared into each other's eyes and chuckled with one another. Overcame a sexy slim thick yellow bone dressed in nothing but a red thong, red bottoms and a black Bettie boo crop top "umm excuse me nigga but these cars isn't going to wash itself; we need your ass back up to the front of the line instead of holding up traffic talking to bitches."

"Hold up wait a minute excuse me" said Fallon, Tripp sticks out his hands and replied "wait a minute Shawty she didn't mean it like that, she cool peeps; look Chi give me 10 seconds." As Chi rolled her eyes and walked away from him and Fallon, he then stood looking at her ass as it jiggled as she walked with an attitude. As Tripp turned back to Fallon he then replied "look I'm going to need you to move up you my next customer", while Tripp tried to walk away from Fallon, she then pulled out a business card to Ladies Nights and replied, " hey if you ever want a sold fantasy you know where to come and maybe if Ms. Thing over there can get her attitude together she may just have a spot in the house with that nice ass booty of hers." As Tripp reached out and took the card from her, he then replied "I'll check it, out now move up."

As Fallon rolled up the window and drove up to the line, she then sat back and relaxed while Tripp and his other coworker started to wet down the car. While Fallon watched the boys go to work on her car and started to soap up the top and the windows of the car. Fallon then noticed as she turned looking out of the window that Tripp's dick print was pressed up against the glass and was blessed with a hook that was on hard. As Fallon continued to take the moment to stare at his dick, he then reached down and grabbed a hold of it in his hands and squeezed it while he pressed it back up against the glass. While Tripp was finished with Fallon's carwash Fallon then waved goodbye and made her way back over to the brothel house. Once Fallon made it back to the Brothel and headed inside to cool off from the scorching summer heat. Suddenly there was a knock at the door, while Fallon placed her purse down on to the desk and went to answer the door. She then tensed up as she paused, as she was surprised to see officer Nathan standing at the door.

As Fallon looked surprised Nathan then waved his hand in front of her and said "hey you ok?", Fallon responds "yes I'm ok but I'm a little confused on how you know where I work at!" Nathan starts to tremble over his speech as he replied, "umm I actually seen you when you got out of your car; I was just passing by the neighborhood", "is that so" said Fallon as she gives him a suspicious look. Nathan chuckles "yes would you like to share a sub with me it's from Gino's", as Fallon sighed and looked back at her desk and back at him, she then replied "look I don't know how to put this but I don't think it's the right time." As Nathan placed the sub back into the bag and stood unsure of what to say next, he then chuckled and said "there goes the sub."

While Fallon stood looking at him mope, she then replied, "you know damn well you didn't get out your car to come over here to split a sub with me so what is it?" Nathan burst out into a big laugh "you know what your right ha, ha that so wasn't the plan; look if you don't want to let me in that's fine, I'll respect that, but just know that if you ever feel that you need to hide something from me you don't have too." Fallon folds her arms as she stepped out on to the porch and replied "what makes you think that I have anything to hide?" Nathan throws up his hands and replies, "I don't know maybe because you kept looking back", as Fallon shook her head at him, she then replied "maybe next time."

While Nathan stood nodding his head he then replied "well next time I was thinking about taking you to dinner; perhaps you'll be my guest." "Perhaps the lady says yes?" said Fallon, Nathan then replies "then I guess the lady done won herself a date." As Fallon looked at him and chuckled, she then walked back into the home and stood with the door cracked open "and when shall this date happen?" said Fallon. Nathan places a smirk on his face as he checked his watch "how about tonight be ready by six", "will do officer," said Fallon. As Nathan said his goodbyes to Fallon an headed down the steps and into his car, he then threw his sub on to the floor of the passenger seat and shouted "fuck" as he sat thinking of his next plan. While Nathan drove himself back over to the detectives unit plotting his next plan, he then stepped foot into the office agitated that things didn't go his way. As Rick saw him walking down to his desk and seen how he tossed his binder across the office. Rick then shouted "whoa dude what in the fuck is up with you", Nathan responded while walking back in forth "she wasn't budging man, I tried to even bribe her with a sub from Gino's and she still wasn't trying to let a motherfucker in." As Rick leaned back in his chair he then replied "damn seems like oh Ms. Fallon is playing hard to get", "very" said Nathan.

As Rick sat up in his chair and turned towards him, he then replied "look this is your girl, you are on this case to find out everything about her so I don't need you messing this up." Nathan frowns his face as he responds "so this is how it's going to be, give me the dirty work so you and the rest of the crew can sit back and collect 40k from a women's activist, it's not that easy Rick." As Rick stood up from his chair and came face to face with Nathan, he then pulled out what looks to be the bill that went against the brothel home in 1975. As Rick held it up to his face, Nathan replied, "and what's that", "that right their son is the bill that went against the Berkley estates, come to find out that her husband Mr. Brad Watson has stolen the bill and hid it from her," said Rick. As Nathan held the bill in his hands and read it to himself, he then asked "wow and where was it hidden", Rick replied, "at their residency in a black binder that was left on a nightstand in their bedroom."

As Nathan took a closer look at the bill and shook his head, Rick then said "this is why we need you to collect any information you can from her and to see if this home is an actual brothel, were looking at 40k split down the middle baby" As Rick waited on a high five from Nathan, Nathan then looked at him and replied "there's no time for celebrations, I need to get to work." While Nathan placed the bill into his bag and grabbed a hold of his slush and walked towards the exit of the office, Rick then shouted "hey where are you going?", Nathan turns around and replies "on a date with the devil." As Nathan turned back around and headed out of the office to go get ready for his date with Fallon. Rick then looked around the office with a smile upon his face telling everyone to get back to work as he cheers in excitement about receiving 40k.

~Arcade~

As the night has falling and money seems to be on everyone's mind, there was one that just couldn't pass up the opportunity to make an extra coin. As Blue lacing up his boots and checked himself out in the mirror, to make sure that he was well put together before performing for the night. He then snatched his phone and stepped out into the hallway to make a phone call to Michael. As he tried making his phone call about two times and didn't receive any answer, he then walked down the opposite side of the hall to use the restroom. While he was heading to the restroom, he then stopped to say hello to the bouncer and to get his opinion on his outfit. As the bouncer told him that he looked great "sexy as usual baby" he then took his compliment and headed down to the men's room. While Blue was passing by a couple of booths and supply closets, there was one booth that stood out to him as the sounds of sex came echoing from it.

While Blue heard the sounds and noticed the booth door being left cracked open, he then walked over to the door and decided that he would close it. As the sounds of a man being pleasured from the back became aggressively loud. As Blue stood listening to the grunts of the man doing the fucking and the sounds of the chair scraping the floor while being fucked out. He then begun to laugh to himself as he thought that it was funny, as Blue waved to the bouncer to come take a listen. The bouncer hurried to the door and replied "when I tell you that nigga is animal honey he is an animal; he comes up in here every other Friday just to fuck him out some bussy." Blue laughs and says "you got to be joking", "shit I wish I was bitch but I'm telling the truth; I sure wish he can bend me over and clap my cheeks like that, have me giving that nigga half of my check" said the bouncer. As Blue and the bouncer busted out in a hysterical laugh while trying to be quiet so they could hear the two men going at it.

Blue then decides that instead of closing the door that he would checkout the man that was slanging the dick. As Blue cracked back open the door and eased his head in to get a good look. He then caught the back of the man's head as the sex worker was crouched down giving the man a blowjob. As Blue watched on and covered his mouth so he wouldn't laugh, he then noticed that the man looked oddly familiar. While the man was coming close to nutting and told the dude that was crouched down throating his dick to swallow his kids. Blue then happened to look harder at the man as he noticed that his voice sounded familiar. Once the mouth of the dude was getting the man wet so good that he was off balance, the dude then pushed him into the wall while placing himself down on his knees and continued sucking. As Blue watched on and jumped back due to the intense push that the man has giving him, Blue then stepped back and looked even closer at the dude that was about to cum. While Blue caught the side of the man's face as his mouth was open and loving every moment of the head job that he was getting. Blue then covered his mouth and closed the door as he realized that the man that was receiving the blowjob was no other than his brother Hakeem.

As Blue stood with his back against the door in shock of what he just saw he then walked back to the dressing room to get his mind together, so he would be able to perform. While Blue stood going back in forth in the dressing room he then came to a pause as he noticed what time it was. As he viewed the clock and realized that it was time for him to get some money, he then headed out to his booth and stood waiting for the next customer to arrive. While the signal of a customer was in the room signaled Blue from the top of the monitor, Blue then grabbed ahold of his whip and waited for the curtains to open. As the button was hit for the sex worker to reveal himself and to give a sexy dance. The curtains then opened leaving Blue stunned as he noticed that his brother was his client for the night. As Blue spanked the whip in his hands and came to a pause looking at Hakeem face to face. Hakeem then got up slowly and rubbed his hand against his face while walking backwards to exit out of the room.

As Blue realized that he was making a run for it Blue then caught up to him at his car in the parking lot before he even made it outside of the building. "Going somewhere" said Blue, Hakeem replied "look it's not what you think I thought that I was somewhere that I was going to see some bitches." Blue responded quickly in a sharp tone "nigga please I don't know who you think you are fooling; but everyone in town knows that sensations is the place where the boys come to play with the boys, so you can save that little wet lie for someone that doesn't no shit." As Hakeem stood quietly looking guilty of his awareness, Blue then asked "so how you liked it?", Hakeem raises his voice "man what's to like about it I only been there for 5 minutes, until I seen you I bounced. Blue gives him the side eye as he knows the truth on what happened behind the doors of booth 11. Blue replies, "Hakeem give it up your horrible at being discrete and trying to convince me that you weren't in booth 11 getting your dick sucked up by some nigga." As Hakeem looked behind him and glanced around the parking lot he then replied "ok look you win, it was me so what if I like getting my dick sucked by a couple of niggas time to time." Blue interrupts him and replied "let's not just say that you like getting that pole wet up by some throat; because to me it seems like you like to dig out as well from the looks of it." As Hakeem placed his elbows on to the top of the car he then looked over at Blue and said "so this is your world huh?", "and that it is" said Blue.

While Hakeem continued to look at him he then sucked his teeth and replied "look you can't tell nobody about this", Blue responds "oh you don't have to worry about me saying nothing; it seems to me that you are doing a great job at hiding that secret, I wonder what other skeletons you have stashed in your closet." While Hakeem opened the car door and turned to look at Blue he then replied "look bro I apologize for what I said I think I missed understood all I know is that I never meant to hurt you." As Blue rolled his eyes and looked away while chuckling to himself he then stepped to Hakeem and replied "missed understood maybe , but hurt never; but I tell you what! the only person that you need to be worried about hurting is Jada because that may be one broken heart that you can't fix." As Hakeem stood nodding his head and whispering "she can't find out about this." Blue then shut the car door and untied his robe and replied "well excuse me as I go make my coin the time is dying down and a bitch got bills to pay and by the way how does it feel to be the faggot now?" As Blue walked away from Hakeem and headed back into the building laughing, Hakeem then opens up the car door and slams it shut as he shouted "fuck" as he dropped down on to the side of it with his hands over his head.

~Dale's Bar & Grill~

While Hakeem sat on the side of the vehicle thinking of how to keep his secret to himself, Officer Nathan was off to crack a secret of Fallon as he invited her out for a couple of drinks and a plate of food. As the pair sat together at a table for two, they both gazed into each other's eyes as they took a sip of their wines. While Fallon placed her glass back down on to the table she then reached down into her purse and pulled out her lip gloss to reapply to her lips. Once she started reapplying her gloss to her lips she then replied "so are we just going to continue to stare at one another or are we going to have a decent conversation." As Nathan begun to laugh, he then said "well, I was just waiting on you to make the first move", Fallon replies, "a lady should never make the first move that's for you to do; I take it that you haven't been on plenty of dates." As officer Nathan turned his head and looked in the opposite direction snickering, he then looked back at her and said "okay you got me I'm really not the dating type", "then what type are you" said Fallon. Nathan takes a sip of his wine and replies "more of the in and out dude", "oh so more like a hit it and quit it; so, my question to you is why we here?"

Officer Nathan places his glass back down on to table and replied "maybe because I see that you're not that type of girl", "I don't think you know what type of woman I am" said Fallon. As Nathan sat back in his chair he then replied "well maybe you can help me find out; we are on a date so help me get to know you better." While Fallon sat sighing to herself, she then gave in and said "Detroit is my home, when growing up the only people that were in my life was my mother and my sister, my grandmother passed away from leukemia and I attended Cathedral and graduated while being part of the honors society." As Nathan stops her, he then replies, "wait you were a geek!", Fallon responds "hey a girl loved her education ok." As Nathan and Fallon both laughed together, he then told her that she can continue on with her story. While Fallon was about to continue on with her story in came the waitress with their dinner and another bottle of wine which was marked as on the house. As the waitress placed their plates down on to the table in front of them, she then looked at both of them and said "you guys look amazing together would you guys mind if I took a picture of you guys together."

As Officer Nathan looked over at Fallon and seen that Fallon seemed to be a little dismissive, he then tried to persuade her into taking the photo by saying "ahh come on this our first date, first date equals first photo." As Fallon rolled her eyes at him and gave him the cutest smirk she then replied "ok usually I don't do this but just because it's you I'll take a picture with you." As the server cheered them on and they moved in closer together she then snapped the photo from his cell phone and admired their beauty together saying that they were a match made in heaven. As the server handed over Nathans phone back to him and walked off, Fallon then snatches the phone out of his hands and replied "I guess we do look good together, don't mind if I send this photo to my phone." When Fallon handed him his phone back and went to dive into her lobster and garlic mash. He then stared at her and at the picture and said "you are so beautiful", as Fallon told him thank you and referred him to be handsome. He then moved his foot over to her foot and begun to play footsies with her, as Fallon felt his foot touching up against her leg. She then stuck her hand underneath the table and slapped his foot from off her legs screaming "oh my gosh that is so disgusting please don't do that again." Nathan then replies, "damn girl you got a strong ass hit" as he held on to his leg.

As the night was coming to an end and Nathan and Fallon were enjoying their dinner date underneath a candlelight and a plate of chocolate mousse. They then sat and talked about memorable moments until they decided to head home. As they left from the restaurant and headed back over to his house, Nathan then escorts her over to her car. As she held on to her car and tried to keep her balance, she then started to laugh loudly as she said "oh my gosh I am so drunk right now I can't even hardly stand." As Nathan begun to chuckle right along with her, he then insisted that she stays a night instead of trying to drive back home. As she took him up on his offer and held on to his waist as he walks her up the steps and into the home. Fallon then quickly falls on to the couch and tells him to grab her some water. As Nathan ran to grab her a bottle of water, he then came back into the living room and told her that he was about to go freshen up. While he passed her the bottle and headed upstairs to freshen up for bed. Fallon then takes a sip of the water and eases back on to the couch closing her eyes hoping to get some rest.

While Nathan was in the middle of his bedroom stripping out of his clothes down into his boxers, he then happens to look at the mirror on the wall and realized that Fallon was standing behind him naked. Once he saw Fallon in the mirror and became frightened, he then turned around and licked his lips as he liked what he saw. As Fallon danced for him swaying side to side while dropping to the ground swinging her hair around in a circle, he then replied "your just tempted to get a brother hard aren't you?" Fallon walks over to him and wraps her arms around his neck and replies, "and if I am would I be able to satisfy you?" Nathan begins to tremble over his words as he stood looking at her boobs and her beautiful gray eyes.

While Nathan looked down at his penis and seen that he has become stiff, Fallon then kissed his lips and told him to finger her pussy. As Nathan went right ahead and placed his two fingers over her pussy, he then begun to penetrate her as she took heavy breaths and begun to moan hard. While he moved in closer to her and inserted his fingertips deep inside of her, while she held on to his neck. She then kissed his lips once more as she pushed him on to the bed and begun to ride him. As Fallon placed Nathan's dick inside of her and made him rub on her boobs as she went up and down. Nathan then grabbed around her waist and showed her who was really in control as he begun to dick her deep. As Fallon moaned and moaned while rubbing the back of his head while he placed her into a different position. She then woke up to water being splashed into her face by Kardea shouting "now boss it's time for you to wake your ass up; you been sleep all day and you got work to do get up." As Fallon woke up from her wildest dream and sat up on to her love seat thinking about what has happened last night. She then stood up and headed into the shower once she noticed the nut stains that ran down her legs.

Chapter 12. Playing by the book

As Fallon headed downstairs into the kitchen to grab her a bottle of water Kardea and Miracle both stood up at the kitchen island staring at her as she walked by. While Fallon stood taking a sip of her water and walked off into the front of the brothel, Kardea and Miracle then followed behind her. With Kardea asking her questions about her night out with Officer Nathan, as Fallon sat down at her desk and taking another sip from the bottle of water. She then noticed that Kardea and Miracle were both standing at the foot of her desk with the biggest smirks on their faces. As she saw both of them grinning while looking down at her, she then replied "oh gosh and how may I help you two?" Kardea laughs and replies "so me and my girl here we would like to know how was last night", as Fallon looked at both of them and rolled her eyes she then replied "what last night because I recall that I was in my master suite." As Miracle frowned up her face at Kardea and shrugged her shoulders she then replied back to Fallon "yea that you were but how do you think you even got back from your date?"

While Fallon sat thinking about her night out with Officer Nathan Kardea then replied "damn girl the night must have been hell of good if your ass can not remember what happened." As Fallon spent around in her chair, she then looked at Miracle and Kardea and replied "it must have been the wine, that red wine must have really knocked me on to my ass last night." Kardea chuckles as she responded, "more like knocked on to some dick, girl you should of seen how your ass came up in here; you came up in here so drunk that Miracle didn't have no clue on what to do with you so she ended up calling me." As Fallon looked over at Miracle in disbelief, Miracle then replied "it's true boss lady you were pretty shit canned", "and let's not forget about the cum that done dripped and dried up between and down her legs" said Kardea. As Fallon shouted "no way" Miracle and Kardea busted out into a big laughter and replied "yes way", as Fallon sat back in her chair clicking a pen that sat in a mug on her desk.

She then looked at both of the girls and busted out into a big laugh saying "ok although I don't remember half of the things that went on that night I have to say that I do remember the sex and having great lobster." As the girls rushed to take a seat to hear Fallon talk about her night out, Kardea then plopped into a chair and replied "girl say no more because I would love to hear about this." As Fallon started to chuckle, she then replied "let's just say that the dick was definitely better than the lobster although the lobster did come with the greatest butter sauce of them all." As Miracle sat with a smile on her face she then shouted "but what about his sauce was it as great as the butter sauce", "yea was it" said Kardea.

As Fallon told them to calm down and to let her tell her story she then said " let's just say that he was a nice guy and that after dinner we have went back to his house and we made a little fun of our owns; the meat was perfect and the experience was tremendous I wish that it never came to an end." While Kardea sat and turned towards Miracle and then back at Fallon she then replied "shit by the way you guys were fucking here, me and her both thought it would have never ended." Miracle replied "yea our ears were literally bleeding from all the cake clapping's and the yes sir's that's been screamed out multiple times", "speaking of yes sir, I thought you said no officer's looks like Ms. Boss lady done slipped up" said Kardea.

As Fallon sat with one hand upon her forehead she then said to herself and the girls "oh no, how long was he here for", Kardea replies "long enough that, that ass was having a hard ass time moving", "girl if a man was to dick me down that good I probably would miss a day of work too" said Miracle. As both of the girls laughed Fallon then told them that she would need a minute as she quickly ran outside of the home to make a phone call to Nathan. As Fallon dialed his number and waited for him to answer while breathing in some fresh air. she then received an answer as he picked up the phone

Officer Nathan: "hello this is Officer Nathan speaking"

Fallon: "Nathan hey this is Fallon"

Officer Nathan: "Fallon the beautiful how may I help you"

Fallon: "I just wanted to check in on you; I see that last night was a wild night, seems to me that we kind of got carried away"

Officer Nathan: "and hopefully you are not calling to apologize; I haven't had that much fun in two years, hopefully by me saying that doesn't make you concerned or a little uncomfortable because I actually enjoyed it"

As Officer Nathan clicks away at his pen, chuckling while twirling in his chair at his desk Fallon then replied

Fallon: "I guess that goes for the both of us, but look I just wanted to tell you thanks for last night I truly had a blast"

Officer Nathan: "it was definitely a time to remember"

As officer Nathan and Fallon sat on the phone during an awkward pause in their conversation Fallon then questions Nathan about being in the brothel home

Fallon: I wasn't going to bring this up but since you were in here anyway, I guess it makes no sense for me to hide it anymore

Officer Nathan sat up in his chair as he waits on her to say what she has to say.

Fallon: what all did you see? When you left out for the night

As Officer Nathan looked around the office to make sure that nobody was paying any attention to him, he then replied in a low tone

Officer Nathan: "look Fallon if you think it's going to be my job to judge you and report you to our detectives unit then you got the wrong guy, I'm not out to get you but I know some guys that would be"

As Officer Nathan sighed and scratched the tip of his head he then said to Fallon

Officer Nathan: "I may have seen a lot but you're ok with me, I actually look forward to seeing you again, if that's ok with you"

As Fallon sat quietly listening to Officer Nathan, she then declined his offer and said,

Fallon: "Nathan I really had a great time with you, but this girl here doesn't do cops"

As Officer Nathan was getting ready to speak, he then heard a click on the other line as Fallon decided to end the call with him. While he sat to himself at his desk, he then threw his pen at the computer screen and sighed while looking into her file. As Rick came walking back down to his desk, he then happens to look over at him and replied "ahh come on now you were just in a great mood earlier, why the long face buddy." As Nathan spun around towards Rick in his chair he then replied "you know it really feels great to score but when you score to deep is when you start to feel like you have nothing else to accomplish." As Nathan stood up from his chair and shook his head at Rick, he then walked out of the office to get some fresh air. While Nathan was dealing with the emotions of falling for Fallon, back at the brothel Fallon remained in disbelief as she was shocked that she allowed a cop to enter her brothel. Which led her to feeling as she's been baited for something that he's been searching for.

While Fallon stood up from the staircase and dusted her pants leg off to head back into the home. Suddenly there was a white SUV that pulled up and parked while blowing the horn repeatedly. As Fallon stopped and took a look from the top of the porch to see who it could have been. Out came Chicago and Tripp dripped down in the Burberry walking up the house. As Tripp saw Fallon standing on the top of the staircase knobbing her head and smiling, he then walked up the steps and said "what up boss lady", Fallon responds, "you tell me Mr. Burberry", as Tripp spun around and popped his collar saying "check me out." Fallon then chuckled and told him that she admires his drip. While Fallon and Tripp continued to flatter one another, from the sidelines stood Chicago becoming easily annoyed as she wasn't given a chance to say hello. As Chicago cleared her throat "hem, hem", Tripp then looked over at her and said "my apologize baby, Fallon this is Chicago, Chicago this is." As Chicago cut him off by placing her finger over his lip she then replied "boss lady Fallon I know exactly who she is; she the one that came and got a wash that day." As Chicago let her finger down from his lip Tripp then replied "damn baby you got a good memory", Chicago responds "only the baddest do baby."

  As Fallon stared at Chicago from head to toe checking out all of her assets, Chicago then smiled and replied "so boss lady you going to let us come in and check out your palace or you going to keep us on the porch hot and waiting." As Fallon looked at Tripp and chuckled, she then looked back at Chicago and invited them in "sure come on in." As Chicago and Tripp stepped foot into the brothel, the only thing that they were capable of doing was looking around as they both were stunned by how great the place looked. As Tripp walked over to Fallon at her desk he then replied "this shit bussing right when you walk through; you didn't tell me that you have the honeys walking around with their titties out looking sexier than a motherfucker." As Fallon chuckled, she then replied "let's just say I left that for you to find out on your own when you visit didn't want to ruin the experience for you." As Tripp was amazed by the beautiful women that walked around the brothel, he then looked over and saw that Chicago done made her a couple of friends. As 3 of the babes were complimenting her on her booty and also feeling up on her boobs. As Fallon looked over and saw that the babes were interested in her, Tripp then called over Chicago to Fallon's desk and told her to stand beside him.

While Chicago said her goodbye's to the girls she then headed over to Fallon's desk and stood by Tripp. As she looked back at the girl she then said to Fallon "you sure got some fine ass women working up in here", "that I do, and I see that you like," said Fallon. As Chicago turned her head back to Fallon she responded "more like love", as Fallon took a look a Chicago as she licked her top lip. She then replied "you know what I think that you would make a great fit around here, I was telling Tripp that back at the car wash that we can use a girl like you." As Chicago turned towards Tripp and asked him his thoughts on her being a babe, Tripp then fanned her off and replied "if you want to then the call is yours. As Chicago jumped up and down and wrapped her arms around his neck and placed a kiss on his cheek.

In came Kardea "don't get too, happy because girls that make the cut around here works for what they want; and around here us girls work for stacks and not racks." As Chicago turned towards Kardea she then replied "well a girl like myself has a lot to offer and a lot to collect so I'm sure that Ms. Chicago, me, she, myself is going to fit in very well around here." As Kardea looked her up and down she then replied "well we will have to see then", as Kardea and Chicago stood staring each other down. Chicago then replied "um excuse you but I don't mean no harm but who are you exactly?" As Kardea stood up against the wall and looked over towards Fallon she then replied "I guess you done forgot to mention to her who I am; I'm Kardea Fallon's lead lady."

As Chicago shook her head and smiled, she then walked over to Kardea and said "you may be a lead lady for Fallon and these other girls, but you is not for me, a bitch like me always knew how to take care of herself when it came to these streets and these niggas." As Kardea stood face to face with Chicago, Kardea then replied in a harsh low tone "I can already see that you about to be a big pain in my ass", as Chicago chuckled at Kardea's remark she then responded "I'm just giving back to you like you have giving to her." While Kardea stood looking at Chicago laughing in her face and then at Fallon watching on with a closed mouth, she then said to Fallon before walking away "really so this what we doing." While Kardea walked away, and Fallon, Tripp and Chicago continued to discuss her becoming a babe. Tripp then tells Chicago to excuse herself as he has one on one time with the boss himself. While Chicago went to socialize with the other babes and went to get a feel of the home, Tripp then asked about the lounge and wanted to know if he could see it. As Fallon wasted no time grabbing the set of keys to the lounge, she then walked him down and allowed him to have his moment.

    Once Tripp looked around the lounge and seen how it was set up, he then replied "damn seems like you been dreaming big for a while." Fallon replies, "dreaming boy please more like a thought; a thought that I made come true." As Tripp jumped down from off the stage and headed over to her, he then replied in a low tone "you know I dreams; matter of fact I dreams a lot." As Fallon asked him what his dreams consisted of, he then replied "chasing this paper being a business owner; maybe one of these days I'll have a club of my own, have it bussing like yours." As Fallon walked away from him laughing and offering him a drink at the bar, he then walked and took a seat at the bar and said "what's so funny you don't believe me or something." Fallon replies as she pours him and her up a glass of wine "no it's not that I don't believe you it's just that your dream is about being a club owner; my establishment is just a brothel, a house full horny women catering to dudes to sell a fantasy." As Fallon took a sip from her glass, Tripp then replied "you say it's a brothel but to be honest I see more to it; look around you, you got butt naked ass women, sex caves a lounge seems to me like you are running more than just a brothel."

As Fallon sipped her wine and chuckled, she then replied "I guess I never seen it like that", "well let me be the first to open your eyes and help you realize that you got more then you thought" said Tripp. Once Fallon walked around the bar and came to take a seat next to him, Tripp then said "so little mama when you are going to let a nigga come through and help you run your palace?" Fallon puts down her drink and replies "when a bitch feels as she needs some help, as of now this is a queendom and queendoms are never to be shared with a king." As Tripp placed a stack of cash on to the bar he then replied "what about now?" Once Fallon took a look at the cash and placed it into the palms of her hands she then asked "how much is this?" Tripp then replied "your holding about 8,000 right now but if we go into business together we can watch that shit multiply, as we add it to the tips your girls are pulling in every night." While Fallon was listening to what he was saying and holding the cash tightly in her hands. She then dropped the cash down on to the bar and said "look you seem like you have a great mind for business; but I just don't know if this would be the right decision, no offense to you but I started this by myself and I plan to finish it by myself" said Fallon.

While Fallon continued to look at the money she then replied "not to say that a little won't hurt", as Tripp stood behind Fallon and placed his hands on both sides of her hips he then whispered in her ear " what would you do for $8,000, I'm a man that usually plays by the book, but is you that woman." As Fallon sat and thought about what he said she then turned around and became stunned. As he was standing with his pants wrapped around his ankles with his dick hanging down to his thighs. As Fallon stood up from her chair and backed into the bar she then replied "umm Tripp what the fuck is this are you trying to sleep with me so I can take your stacks." As Tripp walked up to her and twirled his finger around her curl, Tripp then responds "maybe if that's what it would take for the boss lady to work with a nigga like me." While Fallon tried to find the right words to say to him down came Chicago clearing her throat and wondering what Tripp and Fallon has going on "hem, hem, hem sorry to break up the party, but it seems to me that yall two been down here for way to long and Tripp we have somewhere to be."

As Tripp pulled up his pants and backed away from Fallon. Chicago then replied "well did she suck it", "nah and stop embarrassing me" said Tripp, as Tripp stood staring at Fallon, Tripp then replied "it was nice talking to you Fallon maybe one day we can work something out." As Fallon shook her head yes and waved goodbye to him while he headed back upstairs, Chicago then stayed behind and walked over to Fallon and replied "I know that he may have offered you 8,000 as a stack but trust me, you dealing with a real one; and one thing for sure is that Tripp knows how to invest and take a bitch to the top, you saying no to Tripp is almost like saying you want to be at the bottom of the grid and one thing about a queen she never wants to fall, that's just something to think of." As Chicago left Fallon with an ear full and a kiss on the cheek she then walked away and recommended that she make the right decision for Ladies Nights.

Chapter 13. Freedom

As the boss lady was stuck in between a rock and hard place on going into business with Tripp, there were two people that came to their own senses. As they realized that they were the opposite of being inseparable. As the car door shut and his pants were half way off his behind, Brad then leaned up against the car to catch his breath and to take another swig of the bottle of Jack Daniels that he drove home with. While he Walked towards the home stumbling over the ends of his trousers, he then managed to open the door with one hand. As he was able to push the door open, he then fell on to the hallway floor spilling half of his drink while trying to pull up his pants. While he laid onto the floor trying to crawl his way towards the kitchen and the living area, he then noticed that Katherine was sitting quietly to herself on the sofa. As he crawled his way to the edge of where the kitchen and living area meets, he then grabs ahold of the bar stool as he uses it to push himself up. While Brad was able to push himself up from off the ground, he then stood at the kitchen island looking over at the back of Katherines head and replied "why didn't you help me?"

As Katherine sat with her legs up on the sofa with a glass of red wine weeping her feelings away, he then waved his hands behind her and shouted "Hellooo why didn't you help me." As Katherine became disgusted with him being obnoxious and outrages she then said "maybe it's because I didn't want to." While Brad walked back and forth in the kitchen repeating the words that came out of her mouth to himself. She then took a sip of her wine and looked back replying, "look at you, you're a mess and you think that I'm going to put up with that every night." Brad yells "put up with what, what's to put up with?" Katherine says in a low tone "if only I had a mirror, I would show you what you look like right now." As Brad walked around the kitchen island and stood in front of her, he then asked her to describe what he looked like while he took a couple of sips from his bottle. Brad becomes hostile as he replied "so what I look like come on tell me what I look like Katherine; since you have all the fucking answers what do I look like to you." As Katherine slapped him across the face and slapped the cocktail out of his hand on to the floor she then shouted "a drunk, a fucking drunk Brad."

Once the bottle was slapped on to the floor and the cocktail wasted out on their adorable white furry rug. Brad then drops down to his knees and laid on to the floor with the bottle and shouted at her "you just don't get me you never have, all you want to do is have it your way; you want to be the captain of everything so bad but little do you know a woman isn't meant to lead in this country." While Katherine stood with her arms folded she then expressed rage towards Brad as she said "a woman is not fit to lead but you sell a home worth a half a million to a woman that runs it as a whore house; that you potentially fucked or should I say you did fuck her how brilliant was that?" As Katherine stood looking down at Brad with a disgusting look upon her face, Brad then gets up from the floor and replied "let's not act like you're the innocent one here there's a lot of secrets that you have kept stashed away." As Katherine stood boldly, she replied "this isn't about me this has everything to do with you and your habits." As Brad stumbles over his two feet while standing and slurring over his words he then said unto Katherine " oh this has everything to do with you darling; do the world know that your pretending to be a woman that values conservatorship, do the people know how much fraud you have committed just to sit in that chair you sit in every day; do the people know that you're a self-centered bitch that hired a racists prick as a assistant that attempted to throw two black men in jail for falsely claiming that they were apart of a home invasion, do the people know that you make a difference out of our son because he's black."

    As Katherine snatched a book from off the bookshelf next to her, she then slams it down on to ground and shouted "Brad that's enough, enough is enough and you know what you said about Isaiah is not true, so you will need to take that back." While Brad stood with a smirk on his face he then said "why should I and who's going to make me, surely not you." As Katherine stood silently with thoughts running through the back of her mind about her relationship with him. She then broke her silence and replied "for years now I watched you scheme, manipulate, cheat and walk around here like some tough guy; for years I watched and allowed you to run freely in the streets and over me but as of tonight I would like to inform you that I'm unhappy." While Brad stood sucking his teeth and frowning his face as he didn't believe a word that she said. She then happens to walk up to him and places her hand on to the side of his face and replied "Brad I am so sorry that you're a fucking douche and that you don't have what it takes to grow up; Brad I would like a divorce." As Katherine removed her hand from his face and slid her ring off to place into the palm of his hand.

Brad then makes his way around the kitchen island into the fridge to grab a beer and replied "wow just like that huh !?" As Katherine remained standing in one spot with the ring balled up into her hand. She then smacked it down on to the kitchen island and replied "and it's just that easy" while walking off to the bedroom. Once Katherine was leaving the kitchen on her way to the bedroom Brad then stops her and replied "Kat I'm sorry", as Katherine turned around and looked at him while shaking her head no she then responded "and what could you be possibly sorry about when you done showed me you don't care." As Brad took one sip of his beer and looked over at her he then said "I'm sorry that I know about your deal and that you don't have a chance of winning." As Katherine stood boldly, she then responded to him with a straight face "you could think that my chances of winning are slim; but I know for a fact that you and your client will get a taste of me. While Katherine stormed off from the kitchen into the bedroom, Brad then walks over to the couch and face plants himself down into the sofa as he was so liquored up to the point that he couldn't function.

While Brad was down and out for the night the ladies back down at the brothel were up and ready to celebrate, as they begun to pop champagne and cheer to Sundays new event stripper bowl Sunday. While the ladies gathered around the table in the kitchen and poured each other up a glass of champagne and made a toast to a successful night. In came Chicago dressed in a sexy lavender silk dress with her hair pulled in a side pony tail waving at some of the babes that surrounded the table. As Kardea saw Chicago being friendly with the other females and Fallon pouring her up a glass, Kardea then shouted out directly towards Fallon "wait a minute now who in the hell invited spoiled honey buns; was this your idea?" Fallon flips her hair as she looks over at Kardea and replies, "that it was, she belongs here as much as all of you belong here; and I hope to see a little more respect for your new sister." Kardea quickly takes a sip of her champagne and places the glass back on to the table and replies "sister girl please, I don't know where you found her; but you best to put her back where the fuck she was found because she is no sister of mine." As Fallon was about to come close to reading Kardea, suddenly Chicago cut her off to come to her defense saying " look bitch you got a lot of nerve talking to your boss lady like that; and baby why are you so pressed when you see me, is it because you know that I can make it rain and all them niggahs wouldn't mind given up them stacks like what is it."

As Kardea sucked her teeth and replied "girl nobody is jealous of your ass and just for you to know again bitch I'm the boss ladies lead lady and I'm sure that your ass can't even get into a position like that." As Chicago rolled her eyes and wanted to know if she was going to stop yapping and start the toast, Kardea then took her hand and shood her away. Once Fallon caught Kardea fanning her to get out, Fallon then takes it upon herself to make the toast for the girls and tells Kardea that she needs to stop. While the ladies drunk up and decided to get a card game going, Fallon then notices that Miracle was missing from the toast and decided to go check on her. While Fallon knocked on the door and entered slowly, Miracle then replied "don't be scared just come on in", as Fallon walked into the room and seen Miracle beside candles that were lit on the floor with a quilt a bowl of oil, a piece of sage and a rosery bead. Fallon then became a little unsure about Miracle as she replied "girl what do you have going on here; you got a girl wanting jump out of her skin right about now." As Miracle told her to take a seat next to her Fallon refuses and told her that she was a little fearful so she would stand. As Fallon asked why she wasn't out celebrating with the rest of the girls Miracle then responded sarcastically "it sure sounds like a lot of fun out there." Fallon laughs as she replied, "girl you already know, that wasn't nobody but Kardea thinking she run shit; she keeps it up I might have to give her ass the boot from being disrespectful."

As Miracle sat placing oiling her hands she then replied, "see that's what I don't like I feel as babes we are sisters, and we should always respect one another; yea sisters argue sometime but we never develop hate for each other." Fallon replies "I know exactly what you are talking about and exactly how you feel as well; sometimes a bond that is broken between a family member could be so toxic." As Miracle looked up at Fallon Miracle then replied "now you see why I'm in here, I rather meditate surround myself around positive energy and cleanse my body as it's been poisoned with toxicity many times." While Fallon smiled at Miracle she replied "I'm proud of you and I'm so happy that you are here safe and sound; now excuse me as I get back to dealing with these chicken heads hopefully they have calmed down from all that hollering they were doing." As Fallon was making her way out of the room Miracle stops her and replied, "so is the new girl really becoming a babe", Fallon chuckles as she responds "what you mean if she's about to become a babe she's already one if you want to come out and meet her you." Miracle quickly responds "no I'll pass I heard the city of Chicago could be pretty dangerous", "well lets just hope that little miss chi town can keep it dangerous with a little touch of playful in one of these bunkers when she finally settles in."

While Fallon cracked a smirk at Miracle and decided to exit out of the room, walking down the hall towards her was no other than little miss chi town herself. As Chicago came to her and thanked her for inviting her over for a toast to the babes. Fallon then smiled and thanked her for coming saying "it was my pleasure and I'm glad that you were able to come by." As Chicago leaned in close to Fallon while Fallon leaned up against the wall, Chicago then spoke in a low tone while unbuttoning Fallon's blouse "if you ever need anything you know where to come and I got you." As Fallon shook her head and replied "yes if I happen to need you I sure will call you but I don't think it would be necessary at the time." Chicago then placed a kiss on her cheek so close to her mouth that she could have locked lips with her. Once Chicago leaned up from kissing Fallon with a seductive smile upon her face she replied, "maybe next time we can toast just the two of us; hopefully you like chardonnay and rose water." As Chicago clutched her purse and walked down the hall of the brothel looking back at Fallon, Fallon then shouted out "will see and waved bye to her."

While Fallon happened to be caught up in the moment with Chicago in came Officer Nathan standing at the front door of the brothel. As Fallon frowned up her face and placed her hand back down to her side, she then walked over to him and whispered in a low tone "look what are you doing here I told you I'm not ever fucking a cop again," said Fallon. As Nathan stops her so she can hear him out she then stood confused as of why he has stepped foot in her brothel. Nathan replies, "look although that sounds hell of amazing that is not why I am here", "then why are you here please enlighten me!" said Fallon. As Nathan took a deep breath and sighed he replied "look I apologize ok I know what your thinking , you think I am this crooked ass cop that wants to go around arresting women due to prostitution; I know that you feel that I invaded your space which I did but it wasn't my doing." As Fallon sighed and rolled her eyes she then responded "well who's doing was it then if it wasn't yours; you seemed a little anxious when you tried to bribe me with a sub but instead you get me wasted fuck me bring me to my brothel and snoop around my place of business." "look" said Nathan, "oh look nothing just get out" said Fallon, as Nathan looked at Fallon and shook his head he then shouted, "look I know your disappointed, but it wasn't me Watson put me up to it."

As Fallon thought about the last name Watson she responded "so you mean to tell me that you are working for that cracker bitch down at the conservative women's committee; I knew it was going to be some shit when she continued to antagonize me." Officer Nathan replies, "she offered Rick and the detectives unit $40,000 just to dig up dirt on you and as of right now Katherine Watson is playing chess now that her and Mr. Watson are getting a divorce; if I was you I would do anything to secure your place of business." As Fallon looked back at the girl laughing and having a good time she then turned back to him and replied "and this is coming from a niggah that was secretly working for the bitch; you know what I think you for the warning but you got to go let me show you the way out." While Fallon quickly walked over to the door and opened it so officer Nathan could be on his way. Officer Nathan then walked over to the door and handed her the court papers and replied "just know that I never meant to hurt you, all I wanted to do was save you and that's because I started to care about you." While Nathan walked off of the porch and headed down to his car, Fallon then closes the door behind him and drops to the floor with her back against the door contemplating on what she should do next.

~Courthouse~

While the date at the courts have been set and the judge was ready to knock his gavel against the wooden desk. In came Katherine Watson with the women's committee holding big smiles upon their faces as they entered in coordination and took a seat. As Brad sat looking at her from the opposite side of the bench, he then started to crack up laughing as he found her coordination to be extremely extra. Once Katherine saw him snickering away at her she then bit her bottom lip and replied, "the only one that should be laughing right about now should be me", "and why should I believe that?" said Brad. Mrs. Watson laughs as she turned towards Brad and says "because you're a fraud and frauds shall be dealt with in the court of law; so please excuse me while I take this moment with my peers to marinate on this sweet victory that is coming our way." While Brad sat watching the ladies of the committee laugh onto themselves, he then got up from the bench and leaned over while whispering in her ear "if you think that you're winning this case you better think again", Katherine quickly responds "or else."

As Brad stood thinking of what to say to Katherine in came Fallon and the babes taking their seat to the right hand side of the courtroom. While the babes took their seats and side eyed the committee, the committee then turned away and started to mind their own business. As Katherine looked over and saw that Fallon was sitting front and center of the courtroom she then replied "oh look who it is you have come at the perfect time; please take my husband, oops I mean my ex-husband back on over to the opposite side I'm sure he wouldn't mind sitting next to you girls." As Brad walked away from Katherine and went to be seated, Fallon then replied "if I was you I would hold my breath because you're going to need it after trying to talk your way out of this one." As Katherine sat with her legs crossed and rolled her eyes at Fallon. In came the honorable judge Matthew McGregor, detective Rick McNulty and officer Nathan, as Rick and officer Nathan walked over to the middle row and sat behind Katherine. Fallon then happens to look over and make eye contact with Nathan while he shook his head in disappointment about being there.

    Nathan replied, "I can't do this, this isn't right", Rick looks over at Nathan and replied "you alright bud?" "No, I'm not" said Nathan, as Nathan sat tapping his foot in frustration over the case. Detective Rick then said to him "ahh here we go with you being anxious, just sit and relax", as Nathan did just that. The honorable judge then took his seat behind his desk and was ready to settle the case, calling for Mrs. Watson to speak first. As Katherine stood up from her seat and took center stage, she then looked at the crowd and referred to the day as one of the greatest days due to the victory she could have over Brad and Fallon. As she stood staring off into the crowd she then replied "your honor due to the bill that went against the brothel back in the year of 1975, Mr. Watson deliberately took it upon himself to make a sell off the estates; knowing that it was against the conservative women's committee's values and needed to be signed off by us to be released back on to the market." As the judge took a look at the bill and seen that it has been signed off, he then questioned the signature on the bill "and who's signature am I looking at here Mrs. Watson?" As Katherine told him that it was her mother's signature, he then tilted his glasses as he glanced over at her and said "and how did your mother play into all of this?" Katherine responded "she was the conservative women's chairman which she left me her position when she passed away."

As the judge apologized for the passing of Katherine's mother, he then looked back down at the bill that was passed and called for Brad Watson to take the stand. Once Brad took the stand the judge then asked "so Brad you claim that you're her husband" Brad replies, "and that I am sir", "well technically he would be my ex husband by the end of this month" said Katherine. As Brad looked over at Katherine and threw up his hands saying that he gives up, the judge than turned to Katherine and ordered her to shush "Mrs. Watson I'm going to need you to stay quiet while he's speaking." As Mrs. Watson came to a silence and the judge continued to ask Brad questions regarding the Berkley estates. Brad then answered all the questions in order as the judge presented them, with one question that stuck out to him and Fallon saying if he was aware of him signing the house over to Fallon as a commercial sight. Once Brad looked back at Fallon then back at the judge he then responded truthfully as he said that he was aware of the property being sold off.

As the judge sat back in his chair and called up Fallon to speak, Fallon then rose to her feet and said "your honor I take full responsibility on having Mr. Watson sign for me and I do apologize, for it all I wanted was a place of business something to call my own." While the judge looked down at the agreement and the bill, he then took off his glasses and replied "although selling a home as a commercial sight in the state of Michigan isn't illegal; I rather you guys have taking precautions to secure your business and to make sure that you obey by the zoning law." As Fallon agreed to Judge Matthews opinion she then replied "your honor I would like to also say that on numerous counts I have been harassed by this woman and her colleagues and also searched by detectives without a warrant.

As Judge Matthew seemed shocked about what he was hearing, Katherine Watson then blurted out "you're running an illegal sex dungeon in the heart of this city; so, what do you expect." While judge Matthews looked at the bill and back at Fallon he then responded "so about this brothel you do realize that it is illegal to run a brothel or any type of sex work in this state?" "That your honor I am aware of; but this brothel that Katherine Watson speaks of is not of that nature" said Fallon, Katherine Watson cuts her off as she shouts out "then what is it then because what I saw was a house filled with naked women and men giving up their hardworking money; have you ever thought to think that the money that they are spending on ass and titties could be used to feed their children's."

While Judge Matthews sat back shaking his head at the despicable decision of Fallon and Brad Watson, he then challenged both of them by giving them six months to close the brothel and to have the Berkely Estates back on the market to be sold as is. As Katherine looked over at Fallon and smirked while rolling her eyes at the both of them. Judge Matthew then turned towards Mrs. Watson and told her that he would be disposing the bill that went against the brothel home. As Katherine frowned up her face at Matthews and wanted to know why. He then held up the bill and replied "due to this bill not being signed by you and that this bill is a falsely used bill that was used to terrorize folks this bill will be trashed as of today. While Fallon and the babes begun to laugh at Katherine, Katherine then turned towards Fallon and the babes and replied "what are you all laughing at, you should be laughing at your madam here; she's the real loser in this case with no one to back her, six months sounds great but I'm sure three months and prison time wouldn't hurt would it." As Fallon adjusted her blouse and smirked at Katherine she then replied "you speak about no one backing me well that's where your wrong and I know that half of you all would love to see me fail; but as today your honor Ladies Nights haves two owners."

As Fallon made it be known that Ladies Nights was being ran by her and another person, everyone including the babes happened to look around the courtroom to see who she was referring to. Once the courtroom doors opened and everyone turned back to see who was entering the room. In came no other than Tripp and Chicago walking down the aisle of the courtroom to hand off the new contract for Ladies

Nights to the judge. Once Tripp stood side by side with Fallon and Chicago handed over the paperwork to Judge Matthews. Tripp then took a stand and replied "to all you that may see it as a brothel, to us it's where a woman sales a fantasy, Ladies Nights is not a brothel it's a place of adult entertainment from cave rooms to strip poles to wings being fried on a Friday night; so your honor if your going to give the babes six months to close down then I guess your going to have to pull out that pink slip on every other club in the city."

While Judge Matthew looked over the documentations of Ladies Nights and found a check towards the back of the folder that was written to be endorsed into his campaign. Matthew then smiled and closed the contract saying "well it seems as the time is winding down and this case has been a very interesting case; I declare as of today that Ladies Nights may stay open and operate as a gentlemen's club as for Mrs. Watson and her conservative committee I order you to pay a fine of $2,500 for falsify documentation and to leave Fallon and the babes at peace as of now court is now dismissed. As Katherine stood to herself looking as her face done hit the floor she then shouted out at the judge and the whole court room "wait just a minute, you cannot be serious are you telling me that these whores and their pimp gets to walk free."

While one of the babes disliked what she said she then replied back with "trick don't be mad that you and your ignorant ass mob done loss." As Katherine held on to her chest and became furious with the judges decision she then ran up to the podium and snatched the mic while yelling "this isn't fair I'm a conservative woman that values America, that respects her body, that values marriage; I cannot loose, I cannot loose, we shall burn the brothel home." As security rushed in and tackled Katherine Watson to the ground and placed her in handcuffs, Judge Matthews then ordered them to take her to a holding cell for issuing a threat. While the babes and the conservative women committee were heading to the outside of the courthouse. In the courtroom sat behind Detective Rick and officer

Nathan wondering what just happened and if they are ever going to receive the 40k from Katherine to put towards their unit.

As officer Nathan excused himself and walked out to the outside of the courthouse and found the babes jumping to a celebratory moment. He then looked over at Fallon as she stood staring him down and gave her a thumbs up as he walked the opposite way. As Kardea and Miracle stood off in the distance from the other babes of the home. Kardea then replied "I can't believe her ass done sold herself out like that", Miracle then replies, "Chicago could sometimes be a dangerous place." While Kardea and Miracle stood unsure of why Fallon would need to go into business with Tripp, behind a holding cell was Katherine Watson trying to convince Judge Matthew McGregor that she Is not a violent person. As Judge Matthews stood shaking his head as he saw through the hatred, the lies and the deceitfulness of Mrs. Watson he then replied "you know Mrs. Watson I heard a lot about you over these past few months and I would like to let you know that even a scornful woman has her day; lets just pray and hope that life doesn't crack your face because it looks like I'll be seeing you soon." As Katherine shouted "for what I haven't done anything wrong", Judge Matthews then looked at her and replied "oh really, so shall I ask your partner here that done filled me in on your schemes?" As Susan McCain came around the corner of the holding cell clutching her purse and smiling at her. Katherine Watson then paused as Ms. McCain looked at her and replied, "let's talk embezzlement shall we."

~The penthouse~

While Mrs. Watson was in a tight spot with the law, and others were out celebrating a victory. Fallon was off to a new start as she and Tripp were off to do business. As Tripp put on some music and popped a bottle of champagne and poured him and her a glass. He then made a toast to new beginnings and new business partners. As him and Fallon made their toast and drunk up, Tripp then fell back on to the sofa and said "you know I really thought you wasn't going to give a niggah a chance." As

Fallon looked over at him, she replied "well sometimes in life things do change and people are giving opportunities." While Fallon took a seat on the sofa across from him and sipped her glass of champagne. Tripp then said to her "well I guess a lot of things are about to change now that we are partners; who would of ever thought that a niggah like me would be running a brothel." As Fallon choked on her champagne as she chuckled at Tripp's comment, she then replied "now don't be running around town big headed now because there is still one sheriff in town and that's me."

As Tripp laughed at Fallon's response, he then took another sip of his champagne and replied, "look you don't have anything to worry about, but can I ask you; what is a queen without her king?" Fallon takes a look at Tripp and replies, "a bitch that rather build her own kingdom instead of building it off the backs of a man." As Tripp sat back on the sofa and chuckled, he then pulled out his stash and begun to roll a couple of blunts. As he begun to roll up in came Chicago in a mesh body suit with a glass of champagne of her own. While Chicago took a seat on the side of him, she then grabbed ahold to one of the blunts that were already rolled and lit it with a match. While Chicago placed the blunt to the base of her lips and inhaled, she then handed over the blunt to Tripp while delivering a kiss to the side of his cheek. As Fallon watched Tripp take a hit of the blunt, Chicago then said to her "oh you going to get a hit trust me", once Tripp was done locking his lips to the rim of the blunt. He then handed it over to Fallon and told her to keep it as he continues to roll some more.

Once Fallon got ahold of the blunt and sat with it in her hands, she then placed her lips to the rim and inhaled. As she did just that Chicago then made her way over to her side of the sofa and sat beside her. While Chicago and Fallon went back and forth sharing the same blunt, Tripp then sat back looking at both of them and replied "you know the way you two got your lips locked around that blunt got me feeling some type of way." As Fallon passed the blunt over to Chicago and looked over at Tripp. Tripp then stared at her undressing her with his eyes and replied "you know I think we are going to do well as business partners, but a niggah like me need to know if you really down or not." Fallon sucks her teeth as she replied "excuse me are you really asking me if I'm down, it's more like the other way around playboy; you went into business with me not me going into business with you." As Tripp sucked his teeth and started laughing, he then replied "looks like that $8,000 is going to pay off huh?" Fallon responds "as long as its handled in the right order of doing business then their should be no problem."

While Chicago sat listening to both of them speak about business plans, she then happened to get up and turn on some music of her kind and begun to twerk. As she begun to twerk, she then poured up Fallon another glass of champagne and offered her to twerk with her. As Fallon couldn't resist Chicago, she then stood up from the sofa an joined her as Tripp sat back and watched them celebrate. While Tripp was siting back watching them throw their asses in a circle, Tripp then excused himself from the room and headed down into the bedroom. Once the girls got enough of twerking, they then headed over to the loveseat and took a break. As Fallon sat admiring Chicago's twerking skills and her banging catsuit, Chicago then placed one hand upon Fallon's thigh and begun to squeeze gentle as she thanked her. While Fallon looked down at Chicago's hand and saw that it was climbing slowly up her skirt, she then placed her hand over her hand and removed it gently as she gave her a smile. As Chicago smiled back at Fallon and flipped her hair, she then said to her "maybe one day", as Chicago tensed up and became nervous about showing affection towards Fallon. Fallon then said to her "you know that is one thing I never thought that I'll do", Chicago responds "and what's that beautiful."

Fallon sighs as she sighed replied "you know fuck around with girls; like it crossed my mind time to time but I never made any attempt to pursue in it." As Chicago turned and stared into Fallon's eyes she replied "this shit just comes naturally it's all about what the heart wants and what the body needs to be satisfied; and if a niggah isn't willing to give us that desire, bitches like us will find it anyway anywhere how and most of the time it doesn't take a dick to get the job done." While Fallon chuckled and Chicago reached over and pinched her cheek, she then looked Fallon in her eyes once more and leaned in for a kiss. As Fallon couldn't hold back any longer, she then easily leaned in towards Chicago and allowed Chicago to kiss her. While the two begun kissing one another and feeling on each other's boobs. Fallon then stopped Chicago and took a breather, as Fallon started fixing her blouse and placed back on her glasses. Chicago then told her that she would be right back that she was going to check on Tripp. While Chicago left Fallon's side and been gone for a couple of minutes to and hour, Fallon then stood up from the sofa and headed towards the bedroom.

As Fallon got a little closer to the bedroom door calling out her name, she then happened to hear Chicago moaning while she was getting ready to enter the room. As Fallon stood listening to her be dicked down by Tripp, she then became horny as she thought of Chicago eating out her pussy. Once she begun having thoughts about being fucked by Chicago, she then pushed open the door and caught a good view of Tripp hitting her from the back. As Tripp saw Fallon enter the room and stood in one spot to watch, he then smiled at her as he continued to go deep into her guts. Once Tripp pulled out of her and flipped her over on to her back while watching Fallon watch them. He then started to notice that Fallon seemed a little nervous to be in the room while they both were fucking. As Tripp moved out of the way and stood up on the side of the bed. Fallon then looked over at Chicago and begun unbuttoning her blouse as she said "maybe one day would be today", As Chicago looked puzzled to see that Fallon was willing to fuck her, Chicago then stood up to her knees on to the bed and called for her to come over with one finger. While Tripp watched on with his dick on brick he then replied "now daddy got two bitches." As Fallon placed both knees on to the bed and crawled her way to Chicago, Chicago then wrapped her arms around her and begun kissing her. As Tripp joined in from behind Fallon and begun to finger her pussy while whispering in her ear "this what doing business is like."

Chapter 14. The Pier's
~Jada's house~

As the sweet smell of cherry pie roamed the air and wine glasses were being poured to the rim of the glass. Laughter filled the room as Jada and Blue sat over a plate of Jada's grandmother's famous cherry pie. "I am so proud that you came by to have dinner and dessert with me" said Jada, "well how could I not especially after you told me you were making your grandmothers famous cherry pie, I just couldn't pass up on that," said Blue. As Blue reached out and gave her a hug and thanked her for the invite, he then stood up from the kitchen table as she called out for his nephews to come say goodbye. As Blue waited patiently for his nephews to come running towards him, Jada then stood silently to herself and started to tear up. As Blue's nephews came into the kitchen and gave him a hug goodbye, Blue then noticed Jada wiping away her tears and pretending to be ok. While Blue told his nephews to excuse themselves so he could speak with their mother, the boys then ran back down into their rooms and closed the doors. While Blue turned towards Jada, Jada replied "please don't, I'm fine" Blue responds "are you sure about that because to me it looks like you are a little upset about something."

While Jada stood with a worried look on her face, Blue replied "you could talk to me what's wrong?" Jada sighs as she responded "it's Hakeem he just hasn't been home for anything lately and it has me worried; it's like how many movie nights are you going to miss with the boys or how many dinners are you going to decline because your either working late or out with your boys, I just don't get him sometimes." As Jada pouted and took a seat down at the kitchen table, Blue then replied "sometimes it's just hard getting through to that boy; Hakeem can be a bit hardheaded and selfish, but all though that's what we see from the outside, we forget what he carries on the inside and that's a heart." As Jada sat thinking about what Blue said, she then asked Blue about what she should do, blue responds "the best thing that you could do is to just talk to him; communication is key and if you want something done sometimes you have to demand it." As Jada stood up from the chair and started to pick with her fingernails. She then looked over at Blue and said "sometimes I wonder if I'm the only one; there has been a couple of nights when I have been woken up by him going out back to have a cigarette and caught him telling someone that he loved them, other than that I just find him on the phone with Michael time to time which I'm sure your aware of."

As Blue shaken his head no and thought of why Hakeem would be contacting Michael. Jada then said out loud "all I want is for him to be home on time for dinner and to just spend time with the kids a little more." As Jada finished up expressing how she felt about Hakeems absentees to Blue, suddenly Hakeem have made it home from where he was at and walked towards the kitchen. As Hakeem made it into the kitchen and saw that Jada was talking to Blue, he then became almost shock to see him as he replied "Blue what are you doing here?" Jada turns and looks at Hakeem and replies, "oh I invited him over for dinner and to catch up" as Hakeem looked passed her at Blue and down back at her with a smile. He then delivered a kiss to her forehead as she replied "if you're hungry there's some pot roast in the crockpot and a cherry pie covered up on the table." As Hakeem walked over to the crockpot to fix him a bowl of pot roast, Jada then turns back to Blue and replied "thank you for coming this means so much to me." As Blue replied "your welcome and gave her one more last hug before she walks him down the hall to be let out. Jada then stops him and asked "what's the name of that place you said you work at again?", Blue responds "sensations, why what's up you going to swing through and have one of them freak bitches suck on your spots." Jada laughs as she said "no but I may need me a couple of toys, it can really get lonely for a bitch around here."

As Blue insisted that she swings by and get some items to fulfill her fantasy, they then said their goodbyes and headed their separate ways. While Jada headed back down to the kitchen to clean the dishes that were made between her, Blue and the kids. Hakeem then sat back at the table while watching her gather the dishes and replied "why was he in here?", Jada responds "I already told you, I invited him over to keep me and the kids company besides he hasn't been over here in god knows how long." As Hakeem became angry and slammed his two fists down on to the table he then shouted "do it looks like that I give a fuck, I told you that I don't want that nigga in my house and around my kids." While Hakeem expressed anger towards Blue being around their family, Jada then snaps as she comes to Blue and her kids defense.

"Hakeem you have to be fucking kidding me, like how long is this going to go on huh? How long are you going to run around here and taint our children's minds with this bigoted bullshit; Blue is not a faggot, and, in this house, he is loved by all and would be continued to be loved and treated with respect as a human being." While Hakeem pushed his dishes to the middle of the table and stood up from the table, Jada then asked him "and where are you going?" Hakeem replied "to bed somewhere I should have went when I first came through the door." As Jada stood silently and allowed Hakeem to walk off from the table. She then decided to stand her ground as she stops him by shouting out "you don't even deserve any sleep, here I done slaved over a hot stove just to feed your narrow ass just for you to come in late once again and to eat half; niggah please, this bitch is fed up and this bitch is going to bed so dishes are on you partner." Once Jada threw the sponge at Hakeem and walked out of the kitchen, Hakeem then pulled out a cigarette and placed it to his mouth as he looked at his call log and slowly stepped outside to make a phone call.

~Stripper bowl Sunday~

As the night went by and the girls were getting ready for their sets, Ladies nights then begun to fill up as the streets flooded with cars and horny men. As the men made their way up the porch to enter the brothel, they then cheered loudly as they became excited about seeing some tits and ass. While the girls were busy in the back dressing room, making sure that they were groomed up for the night. In came Fallon the boss lady herself, moving quickly and telling the girls to hustle and bustle their butts for the sake of them having a show to do for the night. While half of the women were finishing last minute touch up's to their attire and their faces, Fallon then stood by giving them ten seconds to apply the last little bit of foundation they were about to use and ordered them to be posted up by their rooms. As the girls quickly touched up their faces and adjusted their thongs and tops. They then walked in a hurry out of the dressing room and headed back up stairs to the main floor.

While Kardea and Miracle watched on, Kardea then whispered over to Miracle "isn't she on one tonight", as Miracle chuckled and continued to apply her make up to her face. Fallon then walked over to them and asked "and what are you two heffa's over here whispering and laughing about? I would like to laugh to." Miracle responds "oh nothing boss lady Kardea was just talking about how this color lip makes me look like a clown, so I'm going to go with a different color." Fallon takes a look at Kardea then back at Miracle and replied "hmm I guess", as Fallon stood behind the girls fixing her hair in the mirror right along with them. Kardea then stood up from the chair and replied "and who are you getting cute for the detective or our new boss." As Fallon paused in the mirror and turned towards Kardea she then replied "new boss what you mean new boss there's no other boss around here except for me." Kardea steps towards Fallon and replied "you going to have to prove it then; because that's not what your help is going around here claiming to these niggas".

As Miracle looked over at Fallon and Kardea, Miracle then happens to let Fallon know that she's been hearing the same thing. Miracle replies, "it's true I been hearing the same thing; I guess you done sold us out and it's only been four months, I guess I'm going to have to look for another job eventually." Fallon raises her voice "look yall stop ok, nobody planned to sell Ladies Nights nor stop you guys from getting a bag; I just needed to do what was best for this business and sometimes you have to make deals that you feel would be beneficial." As Miracle and Kardea looked at each other and smiled, Kardea then turned towards Fallon and responded "well tonight I guess we will be dancing and doing a hell a lot of fucking like it's our last; because when a bitch smells fish just know that it's been left out to spoil." "Well Ms. Thing just know that I have a good nose that can pick up any scents; and lately it's been picking up yours let's not forget when you wanted to Fly high in one of my bunkers, yea just know that people do talk."

While Fallon exposed the truth behind Kardea and her drug using, Kardea then looked around the room at Miracle and replied "and I wonder who told." Miracle quickly throws up her hands as she replied "don't look over here because it wasn't me", as Kardea continued to mean mug Miracle she then adjusted her bra and said "girl lets go we got a show to do; and as for you I would be watching my back around spoiled honey buns and her pimp." As Kardea walked away from Fallon and headed out to the stage, Fallon then stops Miracle as she grabbed her arm and replied "I don't know who the hell Kardea thinks she is and I don't know what the hell you two got going on; but I am telling you now don't let her spoiled ass bring you down in this brothel you hear me?"

Miracle replies "yes boss lady", "now you take your pretty ass out there and give these men a show and remember to protect your stacks," said Fallon. As Miracle walked off and headed out on to the stage. Fallon then followed behind her passing by the fellas that came for a dream fantasy and headed back up to the main floor to welcome the men into the brothel. As she reached out for the mic by the stereo system she then held the mic to her face and welcomed the guys in "ohh, gentleman , daddies and sirs I know you guys have been waiting for a while now so let's get this motherfucking show jumping and keep them dollars coming; Hustlers, ballers ,players and pimps welcome to stripper bowl Sunday."

    As Fallon cut the ribbon and moved out the way so the men can come on through, she then made security direct the horny crowd of men towards the lounge and bunkers as they became rowdy while walking through. Once Fallon placed the gigantic scissors into the corner of the waiting room, suddenly she received a tap on her shoulder and a slap on the booty. As Fallon thought it was one of the men that were passing through to head to the lounge, she then turned around ready to give him a piece of her mind until she realized that it was no other than Chicago. As Chicago jumped back so Fallon wouldn't strike her or give her a piece of her mind. Fallon then apologized and gave her a compliment on her look, claiming that she looked unforgettably sexy. Once Chicago saw that Fallon came back to herself, she then took her comment as a compliment and spun around in a circle so she could get a good look at her ass. While Fallon begun gassing up Chicago, Chicago then wanted to know if she has seen Tripp anywhere around the brothel. As Fallon told her exactly where he was at, Chicago then delivered a smile to Fallon and grabbed her by the palms of her hands while luring her up to her master suite.

    While the ladies were off to the top floor of the home, down in the lounge stood Tripp introducing the baddest bitches in Ladies Nights. As he told the crowd to put their hands together and to give it up for Kardea and Miracle. Miracle then hit the stage with a strut to the pole as Kardea dropped down from the pole into a split. As the crowd went crazy and everyone started to throw them stacks, Miracle and Kardea then looked at each other and joined each other on the pole and begun to give the crowd their wildest fantasy that they wished. As the girls made it half way up the pole and sat in a sitting position facing one another both of the girls then took off their tops and threw it down to the stage. As Kardea sat looking at Miracle while Miracle sat looking at her, both of the ladies then cracked a smile and shouted out "let's do it."

As both ladies begun to rock the pole and swing their hair while delivering a few fan kicks, the crowd then went crazy as all the ballers begun to make it rain. As Miracle hung upside down from the pole and saw all the money that has been thrown on to the stage and falling from the air. She then drops down from the pole and begun to start dancing in the money. While Kardea hung from the pole watching Miracle enjoy the feeling of money touching up against her skin she then performed a move called the chair and came down while delivering the carrousel. While Kardea saw that the crowd was lit, and the DJ was spinning the fuck out some of the tracks. Kardea then ran up next to Miracle and started to perform in the money right along beside her.

As the top ladies of Ladies Nights were down in the lounge handling business by raking up some of the biggest coin that the brothel has seen. Upstairs in the master suite was Fallon and Chicago. As Chicago rushed Fallon into the suite without her knowing what was going on, Chicago then closed the door behind her. As Fallon tried to figure out what Chicago was up too, Chicago then backed her into the wall and begun to kiss her. As Fallon pushed her off of her, she then said "whoa wait a minute Chicago; you got work to do don't you suppose to be in a bunker?" Chicago replied "now what would I need with a bunker when I got you, I'm sure one of them lame ass brothers could wait and besides your going to be making plenty of bank from the lounge anyway." As Fallon crossed her fingers hoping that she would, she then looked at Chicago and replied "look although that sounds great I still need your sexy ass in one of the bunkers; one thing I don't play about is my money." Chicago replied "well I guess that's makes both of us we both don't play about our money; but when it comes to me I definitely don't play about my pussy." While Chicago tilted Fallon's chin up, she then looked at her and said in a low sexy tone "and as of now I would like to know do you want it?"

While Fallon removed Chicago's hand from her chin she then responded in a low tone "do I want it? So, this must be why you wanted to know if Tripp was occupied." As Chicago quickly placed her finger up against Fallon's lips she then said "Tripp being occupied is all a girl ever wanted; and as of right now I'm sure that me and you both know a little something about wanting, this time with no interruptions or demands from a male perspective." As Fallon looked around the room and said "so what are you saying that Tripp isn't good enough?" Chicago chuckles as she places both of Fallon's hands in a set of handcuffs and replies, "nah I'm not saying anything like that; but what I am saying is that sometimes a nigga just can't find a bitches spots, but us woman we know what another woman wants." As Chicago backed away from Fallon and twirled around while releasing herself from her lingerie. She then played with her hair and did a sexy dance for her while feeling all over herself while squeezing on to her boobs.

As Fallon stood up against the wall mesmerized Chicago then dropped on to the floor and crawled to her, as she crawled over to her and stood up on to her knees. She then started to feel up Fallon's legs and begun to massage her inner thighs, as Chicago continued to keep rubbing her thighs. She then placed her lips on them and started to kiss in between them as she made her way further up. While she made her way up Fallon's thighs and slid her panties to the side, she then placed her lips on to her pussy and begun to suck on to her pussy lips. Once Chicago gripped and held on tight to Fallon's thighs, Fallon then pent herself up against the wall and begun to moan while rubbing her fingers through her hair.

As Chicago made her way up and unhandcuffed Fallon, Fallon then stared into her eyes while taking heavy breaths and pushed her on to the bed and begun to kiss all over her. As the girls rolled all over the bed and kissed all over each other's neck's Chicago then reached underneath the pillow and grabbed a strap on dildo. As she kneeled on to all fours and waited for Fallon to peg her, she then replied "sometimes girls just want to have fun." As Fallon held on to the dildo in the palms of her hands she then strapped up and grabbed ahold of Chicago's hair and begun to hit her from the back. As Chicago moaned and told her to beat up her pussy,

Fallon then got into her groove and did just that while Chicago managed to cream up the plastic fella and have her taste her nut.

As the girls were off having their own fun, back down in bunker 12 was no other then Blue, showing off some of his impressive skills while he made a little fun of his own. As Blue pulled up his draws and pulled off the bib that was around his neck, he then stood up to his two feet and walked over to the sink to clean off. While the man laid back on to the futon making himself comfortable by kicking off his shoes. Blue then turned around at the sink and walked over to him in a hurry replying, "niggah wait what the fuck do you think you're doing?" As the man was laid back with his hands behind his back wiggling his toes, he then looked up at Blue and said "baby I'm staying here with you; besides a niggah may want to go for round two." As the man that was laid back chuckled and begun to close his eyes, Blue then kicked the couch as he became irritated with him replied, ah oh hell no my dude is you sleep? get your ass up and get the fuck out let's go." As the man got up from the couch and started to fasten his belt buckle, he then looked at Blue with a grin on his face and pulled out his penis while offering Blue for one more blow. While Blue happened to notice his dick hanging from his jeans, Blue then groaned and pushed him towards the door while telling him to get out and that he was high as fuck.

While Blue was able to fish him outside of the room, he then closed the door behind him and went to finish freshening up for his next customer. As Blue heard the door knob turn and the door close behind the person. Blue then adjusted his pilot hat that went well together with his next outfit and told the customer that he would be right with them. As Blue took one more look in the mirror and saw how sexy he looked, he then walked from around the draped curtains and replied "ok daddy are you ready to be flown out." As the man that sat on the futon replied "how about I ask you", Blue then came to a pause and lifted his head up slowly from looking down at the pilot instructors manual, as the voice of the man sounded familiar. As Blue looked up and happened to see who it was

Blue then replied "what are you doing here and what do you want from me?" Once the man licked his lips while checking him out, he then replied "now what type of question is that you know that where ever you go I go and that you owe me what I deserve."

As Blue stood thinking about what the man deserved from him, he then replied "look Daryl if this is about the dance from the bar, then you can just save it ok; them days are over, now can you excuse me as I have other customers to tend to. As Blue started to walk over towards the door to let him out, Daryl then jumped up quickly from the futon. Raising his voice as he chased after him saying "other customers, man if you don't get the fuck over here", as Daryl grabbed ahold of blue's arm and choked him by his throat. He then whispered into his ear as he dragged him back over to the futon and said "don't make me do something to you that's going to have your family and friends wondering what happened to you." As Blue tried gasping for air while Daryl's hand was around his neck, Daryl then let him go as he pushed him and told him to dance. While Blue held on to his neck trying to breathe, while looking at Daryl, Daryl then takes a seat back on to the futon and replied "this is a pretty nice set up they got for you over here, maybe I should request a few services and see where that leads us."

While Blue held on to his neck he then shouted out "it would lead us nowhere, why are you stalking me; what is your obsession with me? Daryl raises his voice, as he pulled out a gun and a stack of cash while sitting it on his lap "So that's how you feel huh? We had a connection something special; but you know what you done with it you ignored it and left to become some midnight tease while you deal with a control freak as a boyfriend." "Leave Michael out of this" said Blue, "oh so that's his name Michael, does Michael know that at one point you were in love with me and that you worked for me transporting and importing molly throughout the whole city," said Daryl. Blue stood nervously as he continued to look down at the gun "we use to rack up lots of cash together we were unstoppable the best in the city; but what happens, you leave me just like the other two times, but this time you left and never came back" shouted Daryl. While Blue stood with his hand over his forehead he then shouted "what was I supposed to do huh? Continue to make money just for you to spend it on yourself and leave me with $50 to fend for myself; look I may not be able to change the past, but I am able to live the future so can you please leave."

As Daryl leaned back on to the futon and threw the cash at him, he then chuckled and replied "that makes up for all the hard times and if you want me to leave, you either dance or provide me one of your services you choose." As Blue stood looking disgusted and afraid of what Daryl could potentially do, he then started to move side by side as he started to dance. While Daryl watched on and lit him a joint, outside of the room passing through with a bag full of cash was no other than Kardea and Miracle in pure excitement about how the night went. As the girls walked the hall and talked about how amazing it was to be on stage, they then handed over their money to security for protection. Once the ladies handed over their stacks, walking over was no other then the co-boss himself Tripp congratulated them on a successful dance. "I have to say that you girls impressed me you guys killed it; did you see how the crowd was going wild for you too, they were on their two feet's throwing Hella bands." As Miracle bounced up and down in excitement she then replied "tonight was so lit like omg we definitely have to do this again, what you say Kardea?"

Kardea looks over at Miracle and replies "tonight was definitely a great turn out and I would be down; but that's only if the boss lady approves of it or not." "Who says that you have to wait on the boss lady to do anything, you guys got me" said Tripp, Kardea responds "we may have you but you're not Fallon, you're just the assistant. As Tripp begun to crack up over Kardea's comment Tripp then replied "so what are you saying that she decided to give me your spot, because last I checked you were the assistant Ms. Leading lady." As Kardea bucked at Tripp, Tripp then replied "whoa, did I make you mad or something", Miracle replies,

"Kardea chill it's not even worth it the joke was petty." Kardea replied, "yea the joke was petty alright, if I was you, I wouldn't get too comfortable around here sooner or later I'm sure Fallon is going to drop your ass from thinking you run shit." Tripp laughs "and this is coming from a hoe that supposed to lead these bitches, but instead she's doing coke in one of her bosses bunker's tragic." As Kardea folded her arms and rolled her eyes at him she then replied "and how in the fuck you hear about that; what did Fallon tell you too." Tripp dust off his nose as he replied "I'm not even going to argue with you Shawty; but just know that behind these bunkers hoes been talking, now if you excuse me I got to catch up with Chicago have you seen her?" Miracle replied "no."

While Tripp walked away from Miracle and Kardea, Miracle then said "girl you got to stop letting people get to you so easy", "that niggah foul I can smell him from right here." As Miracle shook her head at Kardea she then replied "look I know how you feel I sense it every time, but as of now I'm going to have to let that feeling go and see what he's made of." As Kardea sucked her teeth and grunted, Miracle then patted her on the shoulder and headed off to her bunker to make some extra cash. While Kardea stood to herself looking around at all the dudes that were waiting in line to enter a bunker, she then spotted out Sapphire and frowned up her face at her. As Kardea stood frowning her face at Sapphire, she then walked over to her at her bunker and pushed her into the wall. While saying with anger "you bitch did you tell these other bitches that me and you were getting high together?" Sapphire shouts "no not at all I don't even know how they even know that", Kardea shouts "don't fuck with me Sapp did you tell any of these bitches our business" Sapphire slaps her hand from off her arm and shouted "no, I don't even know who is starting the rumor but Fallon came and spoke to me too." As Kardea placed her hands upon her hips and thought about who could be spreading the cocaine rumor. Sapphire then said "I knew you would think it was me but I would never jeopardize our friendship; we came in this bitch together and if we got to get the fuck out we getting out together."

As Kardea sighed and shook her head in agreement with Sapphire, she then reached out and gave Sapphire a hug and told her that she loved her. While Sapphire and Kardea hugged it out, suddenly security let through someone that Kardea and Sapphire wasn't looking forward to seeing. As Kardea opened her eyes and saw who it was, her heart begun to thump hard as she begun to panic. While she was hoping that someone would walk in front of him so she could let go of Sapphire to make a run for it. As Kardea and Reiko locked eyes, Reiko then smirked at her and pulled up his shirt and showed her his gun. While Kardea begun to panic even harder while holding on to Sapphire, Sapphire then let go of her and held on to her shoulders shouting "Kardea, what's wrong are you ok?" As Kardea was zoned out and only heard Sapphire mumbling to her, Sapphire then turned around as she wondered who she was looking at. As Sapphire turned and saw Reiko staring down both of them. Sapphire then whispered to Kardea "bitch we need to leave", "we need to leave asap" said Kardea. As Reiko stood staring them down, he then stuck out his hands and formed it into a gun threatening to shoot them. While Sapphire grabbed Kardea by her hand and started backing up slowly, Reiko then made his way towards them pushing through the crowd in a hurry. As Sapphire and Kardea ran into the back of the house to escape out of the back door, they then ran quickly across the road to get into the car. While Sapphire started it up and was about to make a run for it, there was Reiko standing in front of the car as the lights came on with a gun pointed at them leaving them nowhere to drive off.

While the girls were held hostage behind a drivers and passenger seat, in bunker twelve was Blue dancing for his life just so his ex-drug partner would not have to request any other services or kill him. As Blue stopped dancing and stood looking over at Daryl, Daryl then licked his lips and said "you know you amaze me, here it is three years later and you still know how to satisfy me; but this time I feel like it just wasn't your best." Blue yells "look I gave you what you came here for and that was to give you your last dance now can you please see your way out my motherfucking room." As Daryl jumped up from the Futon and punched Blue in the stomach, Blue then fell to the ground and held on to the left side of his stomach, as Daryl yelled for him to get up "get up, get the fuck up, get the fuck up now."

As Blue stood up from off the floor Daryl then pushed him on to the futon and replied "I bet you will learn not to talk to me like that again." While Blue held on to his stomach while looking up at him. Daryl then looked at the board of services and said "you know you have some interesting services that I don't mind trying; but I don't think neither of them services are better then what you have between your legs." As Daryl unbuckled his pants and dropped his draws, Blue then yelled out "wait what the fuck are you doing?" Daryl replies "just making up for a time that was lost; now let me in on that ass", as Daryl got close to Blue and begun to grab at him. Blue then started to kick him and tried pushing him off of him, as both tussled with one another with Daryl being the strongest. Suddenly there was a trigger that was pulled and a bullet that connected with the back of Daryl's head.

As Fallon and Chicago were through with satisfying each other's sexual desires, in came Tripp on the search for Chicago. While Tripp entered the room and found Chicago laid in bed with Fallon. Tripp then shouts "Yo what the fuck is this yall two fucking or something", Chicago jumps out of the bed as she responds "look Tripp it isn't what you think we were just chilling." "Chilling so you mean to tell me that you two were just chilling in the bed ass naked; Chicago stop thinking I'm stupid," shouted Tripp. Chicago responds "daddy you're not stupid I'm sorry", as Tripp grabbed Chicago by her waist and brought her into his arms. He then replied in a low tone "how many times am I going to have to tell you to stop fucking bitches without me," said Tripp. Chicago looked over at Fallon and replied "it was just a feeling at the moment", as Tripp snatched her by her neck and looked at Fallon. He then replied "boss lady I am sorry that you must see this but next time make sure that little Ms. Chicago doesn't get to frisky; she has a bad habit of doing what the fuck she wants to do." As Fallon got out of the bed and stood on the side of it, she then shouted out to Tripp "let her go; it was my fault I'm the one that wanted it." As Tripp loosen his arm from around her neck he then looked over at Fallon and said "so you the one that wanted the quick fuck", Fallon rolls her eyes as she replied "maybe."

While Tripp stood looking at the both of them he then started to chuckle underneath his breath and replied "I would say carry on then but you need to be in bunker 15 handling your business; just like there's pussy to be ate there's also money to be made." As Fallon stood silently looking on at Tripp telling Chicago about making her money, she then overheard yelling that came from the downstairs area of the brothel and told Tripp to be quiet. As Tripp looked over at Fallon suddenly the sounds of gunshots went off and everyone that was in the brothel took off running. While Fallon, Tripp and Chicago heard the footsteps of people running out of the brothel. They then rushed down to the main area to see who has been shot and to check on the ladies of the brothel. As Fallon asked the babes where Sapphire and Kardea were, the ladies of the brothel shrugged their shoulders as they didn't have any clue. While Fallon thought of anyone else to ask, she then rushes down to bunker 12 to see if Blue knew where Sapphire and Kardea were. As she made it in between the doorway of bunker 12 to ask Blue if he has seen the girls, Fallon then burst out into a scream as she yelled "oh my gosh what the hell is going on here?" As Blue looked at Fallon and saw the fear and concerning look written over her face while looking down at a dead body. Hakeem then releases his hood from his head and replied "let's just say that the niggah had it coming"

As Tripp, Chicago and the other women of the brothel rushed down to see what has happened in bunker 12. Hakeem then looked at Fallon and Blue and said "I have someone that can get rid of the body, but it's going to cost." As Tripp looked over at Hakeem he then shouted "you got to be fucking kidding me man what type of shit is this." Hakeem replied "the type of shit that we call protecting our own", as Fallon stood in shock not knowing what to think of. Hakeem then told Blue to help him move the body to the trunk of his car. While Blue ran to pull the car around back, Fallon then replied "Hakeem there's a dead man laying on my brothel house floor what the fuck done happened?" "I Caught the motherfucker trying to rape Blue; I know all about this cat and let's just say he was a dangerous person." As Fallon stood not believing her eyes she then turned back towards the other women and told them to head home. As they rushed down the hall and grabbed their belongings they then ran out of the house and walked to the nearest bus stop. While Blue made it back and asked Hakeem if he was ready to get rid of the body, Hakeem then shook his head yes and grabbed the dude by his legs. As Blue grabbed ahold of Daryl's arms and started to carry him out of the house with his brother Hakeem. Blue then looked up at Fallon as she stood from the porch and replied "I'm sorry."

Once the body was placed inside of the trunk of the car and Hakeem yelled for Blue to get inside of the car. Blue then backed away and hurried off into the passenger seat and ridden down to the pier to get rid of the body. While Blue and Hakeem made it down to the pier there was a man by the name Walter that was dressed in all black and spoke with a heavy Italian accent. As Hakeem fanned him over to the back of the trunk and opened it so he could take a look at the body, Blue then sat sick to his stomach as he was afraid of the outcome. While Hakeem and Walter grabbed ahold of the body from inside of the trunk, they then brought it over to the ramp of the pier and said some last words. While Blue watched on from the rearview mirror he then stepped outside of the vehicle and walked over slowly towards them and stood in between. While Blue looked down at Daryl's body and shook his head while feeling horrible about the decision that Hakeem and Walter were about to make. Walter then looks at him and replied "any last words for your friend here?", as Blue turned his head and looked at Walter and then back down at the body. He then built up with anger as he thought about how Daryl tried to take advantage of him and decided to spit on him as he replied "dump him."

Once Blue made the last call for Daryl's body to be tossed into the pier, Hakeem and Walter wasted no time as they tossed him in and walked away from the scene. Once Hakeem made it back into the car and seen that Blue was panicking, he then grabbed ahold of his hand and calmed him down. As Blue looked over at Hakeem and replied "sometimes I wonder about who you are", Hakeem then replied "for here on out I'm who has your back that's all you need to know." As Blue looked over at him and at a bottle of brown liquor that he had stashed in between the seats of the car. He then grabbed ahold of it and took a swig to calm his nerves, as Blue took a few more sips of the brown liquor. Suddenly Walter knocked at the window to get Hakeems attention, as he rolled down the window to see what he wanted.

Walter then asked for his cut as Hakeem looked over at Blue, he then said unto Walter what if your cut wasn't in dollar bills, but it could get wet. As Walter thought about what Hakeem was saying he then replied "a rack is what I need buddy but as for now I can settle for whatever." While Hakeem rolled back up the window and sat back in the seat taking a sip of the brown liquor. He then said to Blue "you know what to do", As Blue cut his eye at Hakeem and turned back looking at Walters car in the back of them, Blue then sighed as he opened up the car door and headed over to Walter. As Blue opened Walters car door and took a seat in the back with him he then lit a cigarette as Walter replied "where off too?", Blue responds "anywhere will do as long as we are away from here." As Walter was willing to give Blue what he wanted he then told his drivers to head out as they cruised the midnight streets away from the pier.

To Be Continued...

Made in the USA
Middletown, DE
11 October 2022